"Tell me... then get the hell out of my life."

"Fine," Shepard replied. "As I said earlier, I've been given some information that I need you to confirm. It involves my brother...and you."

Maya shrugged. "There's nothing to confirm or deny. What happened between the two of us took place too many years ago to matter now. What is it you really want?"

"I want the truth."

"I don't know what you're talking about."

"Yes, you do," he said. "When you were a teenager, you took a lover five years your senior. He was my brother, but he was also a criminal who justified his actions in the name of revolution. In the end, he paid for his foolishness with his life."

"He made his own choices," she said stubbornly.

"And so did you. But there's more to the story than that, isn't there?" He didn't wait for an answer. "A woman recently came into my office and told me something. A secret, she said."

Maya's face slowly became the color of bones.

"You know what she told me, don't you?"

"Of course not. How could I?" She licked her lips.

"You're lying." Shepard leaned across the table. "And this is the time for truth. Tell me, Maya, did you have my brother's child?"

Dear Reader,

My husband opened a fortune cookie last week and the little paper inside read, "Stop your search. What you seek is already yours."

I love this message because everyone I know seems to be searching for something—the right relationship, the perfect job, the flawless body.... We're all constantly looking for more than we already have, and I'm as guilty as the next person. Why do we do this?

My mother would have said we're cursed with ambition, and in a way, she would have been correct. Most of us *are* ambitious and we want the best.

There's nothing wrong with this, of course, because these searches make us better people. Sometimes, though, the treasures we seek are in our grasp and we're blind to that reality. We don't recognize what we already have.

There's a corollary to this. I call it the "unexpected treasure." This is when we search for one thing and discover another.

In this story, Maya Vega is searching for legitimacy. She wants, once and for all, to be someone others look up to. What she doesn't realize is that she already has this respect. And Shepard's looking for a truth that he already knows. He's been able to deny the reality for some time, but his eyes are about to be opened in a way he can no longer ignore.

Together, Maya and Shepard begin their search, their pasts interwoven as tightly as a braid. Both come to realize the answers they already knew and then they discover something better, something they weren't even seeking in the first place. They encounter the unexpected treasure.

In all your searches I hope you find the same success. Just remember...be open to unexpected treasures and consider the idea that whatever you're seeking might already be yours.

Sincerely,

Kay David

The Searchers
Kay David

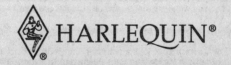

HARLEQUIN®

TORONTO • NEW YORK • LONDON
AMSTERDAM • PARIS • SYDNEY • HAMBURG
STOCKHOLM • ATHENS • TOKYO • MILAN • MADRID
PRAGUE • WARSAW • BUDAPEST • AUCKLAND

ISBN 0-373-71149-2

THE SEARCHERS

Copyright © 2003 by Carla Luan.

Visit us at www.eHarlequin.com

Printed in U.S.A.

The Searchers

PROLOGUE

Punto Perdido, Colombia

"YOU GO IN THERE and tell her the child is dead or *por Dios,* I'll make you wish you'd never been born yourself!"

An inch away from his wife's face, Segundo Alvarez jerked his thumb toward the room at the rear of their shack, his voice as sharp as the axe he carried every day to the emerald mines. "Tell her it's dead then get rid of her. *¿Comprendes?*"

Renita darted a look past her husband to the bedroom. Her niece was lying in a bloody mess on the bed, the midwife, Amarilla Rodriguez, still working beside her. Bringing her terrified gaze back to Segundo, Renita knew pleading for mercy was useless but she had to try.

"Segundo, *por favor*... She's weak, she's sick, she just gave birth..." Renita shook her head, her eyes filling before she could stop them. "I can't throw her out, she's my only family. And I can't tell her the baby died! It's not right to—"

Without any warning, Segundo raised his hand and backhanded her. She fell to the dirt floor with an involuntary cry, biting her lip savagely, the sharp sting of blood and pain flooding her mouth. The taste enraged her, and she glared at her husband, her hand against her face.

"How can you do this?" she screamed. "She's just a teenager! If they find out, they'll kill us all!"

"They won't find out," he said ominously. "I'm going to take care of everything." Stepping closer, he swung his hand up and she flinched, but instead of hitting her again, he jabbed a finger toward the bedroom. "Go in there and tell her. Then make her disappear. I won't have a *puta* like her under my roof! I'm a God-fearing man."

To punctuate his order, he kicked her hard, the edge of his cheap leather boot catching her squarely in the chest. Red stars exploded in her vision but Segundo gave her no time to think about her agony. Instead, he yanked her to her feet, his grip on her elbow the single thing holding her up. His words were hot against her face, his breath fetid. "I'm warning you, Renita. You get her out of here, or I will." His jaw tightened. *"¡Esto me molesta!"*

"But the baby…" she whimpered.

"I will handle the bastard and his father, too." He squeezed her arm until his thumb met his fingers, then he shook her as a dog would a rag. "When I get back, she'd better be gone. If she isn't, I'll take care of her myself and you'll like that even less."

He released her abruptly and she fell to the floor, tiny puffs of dirt rising from his angry footsteps as he stomped out of the house. Stunned with pain and guilt, Renita wrapped her arms around her waist and struggled to recover her breath. Then she lifted her eyes and met the midwife's gaze. Amarilla's blank expression reflected none of Renita's anger and helplessness. She'd seen too much in her lifetime; she knew she couldn't change what was about to happen.

Renita buried her face in her hands and began to sob. The blood-soaked midwife turned to the bed and gently took the young girl's hand. Compared to the women whose children she delivered, Amarilla was old, but the week before, for the very first time, she'd given birth herself and had a new daughter. She didn't have to imagine the pain her words were about to inflict. Her rough voice held sympathy as she leaned over the bed and spoke.

They heard the scream all the way to the square.

CHAPTER ONE

Muzo, Colombia
Eighteen years later

THE EMERALD WEIGHED at least fifty carats, probably more.

Hefting the uncut stone in his hand, Shepard Reyes turned to the window as his helicopter rose into the air. A cloud of fine, black dust, stirred by the spinning rotors, enveloped them, then the chopper gained altitude and escaped the choking darkness. Shepard put his hand against the bulletproof glass and stared into the open pit a hundred feet below.

The Muzo mine was the oldest, largest and most productive emerald mine in the world. And the Reyes family had owned it since the conquistadores had come to Colombia.

He'd seen the cuts across the mountain's top thousands of times but Shepard always had to look. He'd spent years learning the Muzo's secrets and no one else in the family knew the mine as he did, including his brother, Javier, who was in charge of the family business.

The pilot set his headings for Bogota and seconds later the mine was gone, lost in the mountain mist. Dropping the stone into his briefcase, Shepard wished the problem he'd learned of this morning would be as easy to leave behind, but his gut told him it wasn't going to go away. At least not until he made it do so.

The peasant woman had come to his office early, before the miners changed shifts. Her name had meant nothing to him, but he'd politely shaken her hand and directed her to sit. He was frequently approached by the wives or mothers of the men who worked in the mine to settle some kind of dispute or fix some problem they'd gotten into. They knew who the real *jefe* was; they expected Shepard to help and he did. That's how things were done in Colombia.

She'd perched on the edge of the chair and refused his offer of coffee. Waiting for her to speak, he'd put her age somewhere between thirty and fifty—she wore the exhausted look of someone who worked hard…and never stopped. But her clothes were clean, and she had an appealing way about her even though she was clearly uncomfortable sitting before him.

"What can I do for you, *señora?*" he'd finally prompted.

She looked down at the floor and spoke softly.

"You have already done more than I could ever ask for," she answered. "I came here today to do something for you."

"I'm sure you owe me nothing, but please tell me how I've helped you. I'd like to hear your story."

"I have a son who is five," she said. "He couldn't run like the other children and he'd get tired very quickly." With an expression of distress, she put her hand on her chest. "I took him to one of the clinics you opened, and the doctors in Bogota, they operated on his *córazon*..." Her smile transformed her face. "You saved my child's life, so I wanted to thank you."

"I'm glad the doctors could help."

And he was. For years, the miners had suffered conditions no one should have to endure. Neither Javier nor their father, Eduard, had thought their workers needed anything more so Shepard had put up his own money to build and staff the small hospital.

"I want to pay you back, *señor*."

"You owe me nothing." Shepard looked at the files on his desk. Javier's name was on the letterhead, but it was Shepard who did all the work, and it was piling up, even as they spoke. "The clinic is free. No one pays for anything."

"I don't have money to give you."

"And that's fine—"

"I have something else, though."

"It isn't necessary—"

"I have a secret." She ignored his attempt to stop her. "You should have been told about this years ago, but…" She dropped her eyes to her lap and knit her fingers together then looked up at him again. "But I didn't have the courage. Now I must tell you."

Her words intrigued him, despite the work he had calling to him. "Go on."

"Something happened in my village a long time ago and you need to know about it."

With a sudden uneasiness, Shepard stood and came closer to where she sat, taking the other chair in front of his desk.

"My niece had a child." She studied Shepard's face. "He had your look about the eyes, but that's it. He resembled his father more."

"His father?" Shepard's gut tightened. "And that would be…?"

"Your brother, of course."

Shepard closed his expression and rose. He'd been fooled, but she'd seemed sincere, unlike the others who'd approached him in the past. "I don't handle *Señor* Javier's affairs," he said coldly. "If you want help for the boy, go to him, not me."

"You don't understand—"

"I understand perfectly, *señora*." Shepard returned to the other side of his desk. "You are not the first to come here and ask for money, believe me."

She stood up, as well. "I'm not asking for money

and I'm not talking about *Señor* Javier. The boy's father was *Señor* Renaldo.''

His hand on the back of his leather chair, Shepard froze. ''Renaldo is dead.''

''I know that. But he wasn't dead eighteen years ago. He and my niece were lovers and they had a child. He was born the day his father died.''

''Your niece…?''

''Was Maya Vega.''

He sat down abruptly.

Maya Vega.

Shepard had never met her but Renaldo had been infatuated with the girl, describing her in detail, telling Shepard how she'd shared his ways. There would always be a place for women like her in the FARC, he'd bragged. The Revolutionary Armed Forces of Colombia, known to everyone as FARC, believed in equality for all, be they women…or mining scions.

Shepard had come to hate the unknown Maya Vega. In his mind, she represented everything that had been wrong with Renaldo: the recklessness, the irresponsibility, the wild way he had chosen to live. At some point, Shepard had managed to force his animosity into indifference, but hearing her name now, he felt that earlier anger return.

He put his reaction aside and spoke carefully. ''If Maya Vega is your niece, then your husband would be…''

The woman held his stare. There was neither

apology nor blame in her eyes—only an empty acceptance that said she'd lived a life with few choices. "Segundo Alvarez was *mi esposo.*"

Nodding slowly, Shepard rejected his automatic response to this name, as well. He'd hated the uncle as much, if not more, than the girl. He calculated the boy's age, realizing he'd be eighteen now. There had been rumors at one time of a child after Renaldo's death but Shepard had had no luck tracking their source or the Vega woman down. The thought prompted a question.

"Did Maya Vega send you here?"

"No. Maya left many years ago, after being told that her baby was stillborn. That was a lie. I don't know where she is now, but I wanted you to know about your nephew."

If the woman's story was true, Shepard's parents would be beside themselves. Despite his rejection of his family Renaldo had been the favorite son, and his parents had forgiven all his misdeeds. They'd be overjoyed.

Javier would have a completely different reaction.

"Stay here," Shepard had commanded, rising from his chair. "I'm going to open the safe and get some cash for you then I want to hear more about this."

When he'd returned, the woman was gone.

Shepard stared out the helicopter's window and cursed softly. What in the hell was he supposed to do now?

Houston, Texas
One month later

BY 7:00 A.M. Maya Velaquez had already done a full day's work.

She'd had to in order to make up for yesterday. Wasting hours away from her desk, she'd endured breakfast with two county commissioners, a morning meeting with a law professor, lunch with the bar association, then dinner with a group of potential—spelled r-i-c-h—supporters. With no time for her regular duties, she'd had to come in early this morning and deal with a backlog of paperwork. Every attorney in the firm handled dozens of cases, but her load was much heavier. Well-known and well-respected in the legal community, she was in high demand, her time precious. Her life was about to become more complicated, too. A local judge, Marcus Chatham, was retiring early and Maya had been suggested as the person best suited to fill the resulting vacancy.

She wanted that black robe for more reasons than she could ever explain.

She took off her glasses and dropped them on her desk pad. A cold front had blown in last night and a morning rain scratched at the glass, a rising wind accompanying it. Maya hated winter. In Houston, the temperatures never dropped too low, but the dismal, gray days and even darker nights depressed her. With all the extra stress she'd been under, she'd let

the weather bother her even more. Thoughts of
home had slipped in before she could stop them and
she'd gotten lost in the past, thinking of things best
left alone. Of green cathedrals filled with iridescent
parrots…of steep balconies shaded by wild hibiscus…of a man who had lived in the shadows and
died there, as well.

With dogged determination, she reined in her
thoughts. *Now* was not the time to allow her history
to haunt her. If anything, it was more important than
ever that she stay firmly in the present.

As if on cue, a knock sounded on her door. She
looked up to see her colleague and mentor, Patricia
Livingston-Wallis leaning against the frame.

"You were perfect last night, Maya." One of the
founding partners in the firm, Patricia's aura of
power fit her as precisely as her tailored red suit and
lustrous pearls. She was Maya's staunchest sup-
porter and the reason Maya had become a lawyer.
Years before, Patricia and her husband, Franklin,
had literally saved Maya's life.

Arriving in the States with nothing but the clothes
she wore, she'd slipped in the back door of the first
restaurant she'd come to and begged for a job.
Franklin, the owner, had taken one look at her and
brought her home to Patricia. They'd proceeded to
open their hearts—and their wallets—and had done
everything they could for Maya, not the least of
which had been having her declared a ward of the
state so they could then be her sponsors. Using their

influence and power, they'd helped her obtain her green card and finally her citizenship.

Their generosity had overwhelmed her and she'd insisted on paying them back by working for Franklin. By the time they'd offered to "loan" her money for college a few years later, she'd come to love them both, appreciating their work ethic and the determination each of them had to succeed. She'd never be able to repay them for everything they'd done for her, but as she'd gotten older she'd begun to understand that she'd given them something valuable in return. Patricia and Franklin had been unable to have children and helping Maya had fulfilled their own needs as well as hers.

And they were still helping her. Patricia's endorsement was the driving force behind Maya's pending judgeship. Without the backing of someone as important as Patricia, Maya doubted she'd be in the running, despite her sterling reputation.

"The appointment's almost in your pocket, young lady." The older woman beamed at her.

Maya returned her friend's smile. "I hope you're right, Patricia. Time will tell. I have to get the nod from the governor first."

"You will." She tapped the door frame with her nails. "You aren't getting discouraged, are you?"

Maya had learned a long time ago that wanting and getting were two very different things. As much as she desired to sit behind the bench, sometimes late at night when she couldn't sleep, she'd won-

dered if she was making a terrible mistake or a very
smart move. The balance was delicate; it could go
either way.

But Patricia knew nothing of that.

"I'm not discouraged," Maya replied firmly, sub-
stituting a simple concern for her real one. "But the
process does seem to be taking a long time."

"That has nothing to do with you, my dear. These
things simply require a lot of finesse. When Marcus
retires next month—and he will—that vacancy *has*
to be filled. And whoever is behind the bench will
be elected to return next November. Stay fast and
hold steady. You'll get that gavel, I promise you."

With that, the other woman strode down the corridor, the sound of her heels fading as she crossed
the silk rug in the entry and made her way to her
own office.

She should have started on her paperwork, but
instead, Maya turned back to the gloomy window.
Patricia may have made the promise, but until
Maya's name was approved, nothing was for sure.
There were no guarantees.

That was another lesson she'd learned early in
life.

A telephone rang down the hall and someone
laughed loudly. The sounds pulled Maya away from
her thoughts and made her realize she needed to get
back to work, otherwise she'd be at the office until
midnight. Again. Swiveling her chair to the credenza
behind her, Maya opened the drawer that held her

files, thumbing through them until she found the one she needed. As she pulled it out, a voice sounded at her door.

"May I come in?"

Holding the manila folder, Maya turned.

A man stood on the threshold of her office, his hands at his side, a leather bag in one, a dripping umbrella in the other.

Without conscious thought, she stood, the file slipping from her fingers to the floor, papers fluttering in every direction as her pulse suddenly roared in her ears. The man said something else and she heard him, but she had no idea what the words even meant. Her brain had ceased to work and all she could do was stare.

SHEPARD REYES HAD always wondered what his brother's whore looked like.

Now he knew.

They stared at each other, the luxurious office shrinking until there was barely enough air to breathe. Dark eyes. Black hair. Full lips. A straight nose that belied her ancestry. Her expression was so fierce and commanding that he could easily imagine her choosing the same lifestyle as his brother. With equal detachment, however, Shepard could see why Renaldo had been attracted to her. She was more than simply attractive; her eyes pulled a person closer and wouldn't let go.

His voice was low and contained and gave away

nothing of what he was thinking. "Are you Maya Vega?"

She swallowed and her throat moved. His eyes went to the motion, then she spoke, pulling his gaze back up. She'd recovered her composure so quickly someone other than Shepard would not have even noticed it'd fled.

"Who are you? How'd you get in here—"

Uncovering the whereabouts of Maya Vega—now Velaquez—had taken more money and more time than he had anticipated but Shepard had been forced by his conscience to hunt her down. She was the one person who could confirm or deny the peasant's story, and if it turned out to be true, then he would be spending even more time and money. He had no patience left for the niceties.

"I told your secretary we were old friends. And you know who I am." He paused. "My name is Shepard Reyes. Renaldo Reyes was my younger brother."

Sweeping up the papers she'd dropped, then dumping them on her desk, Maya Vega stared at him. Her demeanor was steady but her expression held fear, and her ivory skin was pale.

Shepard felt a twinge of sympathy that he immediately squelched. If everything he knew about her—and half of what he suspected—was the truth, then she deserved nothing but his scorn.

"What do you want?"

"I need to talk to you," he said. "Something has

come to my attention that no one but you can confirm. If I could have some of your time, I'd appreciate—''

"I'm sorry, but that's impossible." She interrupted him and tilted her head toward the hallway.
"You can talk to my secretary on the way out. Perhaps next week sometime…"

Their gazes locked, the knowledge flowing between them that she would be "booked" until the
end of time…at least as far as he was concerned.

He ignored her obvious brush-off. "You do remember my brother, don't you?"

"Of course, I remember him." If she was this
cool in front of a jury, he could see why she was in
the corner office. "But what happened back then
took place in another lifetime. What could you possibly want with me now?"

"That's what I'd like to discuss. If you'd accompany me to breakfast, I'll explain."

"I don't have time for that. You'll tell me why
you're here right now and then you'll leave." The
words came out hard and flat. "Talk or walk."

He understood exactly what she was doing; in her
office, she held the power. If they went somewhere
neutral, they'd be on even ground.

"The issue is too involved to be explained in five
minutes."

She glared at him stonily. "Then I guess it won't
be discussed at all. I'm not leaving. I have appoint-
ments I can't break."

Anger flooded him. He didn't want to do this the hard way, but he could if necessary. "I'm sure that *would* be best—for you. But that's not going to happen."

"And if I refuse to cooperate?"

"I don't think you want to do that."

"Is that a threat?"

"Not at all," he said. "It's simply the way things are. If I were you, I'd accept that. Otherwise I might be forced into looking elsewhere for help."

She didn't blink and she didn't speak.

He nodded toward the rolled-up newspaper lying on the edge of her desk. "I'm sure the press would be delighted to assist me. It's not every day a former leftist guerrilla aspires to become a judge."

CHAPTER TWO

MAYA WENT COMPLETELY STILL and stared at the man before her.

He smiled, his calculating expression as cold as the fear that suddenly possessed her. "All I want is a small portion of your time…and the truth," he added. "Then I'll leave you alone and you'll never see me again."

"Is that a promise?"

He actually seemed to consider his answer before he nodded. "You have my word."

She felt as if she'd swallowed broken glass. Since the day she'd left Colombia, she'd worried that this might happen. She'd done everything she could to prevent it…in fact, her life had been designed to keep her past in the past, but if Shepard Reyes had found her, then she'd clearly failed.

Before she could say anything more, Patricia suddenly appeared in the doorway. Maya felt the blood drain from her heart and pool in her stomach.

He turned and spoke pleasantly. "Hello there."

Maya crossed the room and came toward them, praying her legs would hold her up a little longer, her mind shuffling through the possible lies she could concoct, rejecting them until she came to one that sounded halfway plausible. "Patricia, this is an…associate, Shepard Reyes. Mr. Reyes…" she swallowed, then spoke quickly to cover her hesitation "…is co-counsel on a case I'm handling for some clients in Mexico." She sent a warning gaze in Shepard's direction. "This is one of my partners," she said. "Patricia Livingston-Wallis."

In her standard intimidating way, Patricia eyed Shepard up and down—then she smiled and extended her hand. "It's nice to meet you, Mr. Reyes. Did you fly in this morning?"

"Yes," he replied in English. "I did. It's always a pleasure to come to Houston, so I take any opportunity that I can. I visit frequently."

He had no accent, Maya realized suddenly, and then she remembered. He'd been educated in the United States at the University of Miami, the long forgotten detail popping into her head. Renaldo had derided his older brother's capitalist choice of a business degree.

Patricia responded to Shepard's charm like a young girl. "Who are your clients, Mr. Reyes?"

Maya wanted to let him dangle, but she couldn't. Who knew what the man might do? "It's Sanchez vs. Sanchez,'' Maya supplied. "It was a probate case we handled a few years back.''

Patricia frowned for a second. "I don't remember that particular case.''

Maya started to answer but Shepard turned to Patricia, his expression so sincere and polite, Maya found herself gritting her teeth. "*Señorita* Velaquez and I were about to go out for coffee,'' he interjected. "Why don't you come with us and I'll explain the situation in detail. I'm sure you'd like to hear all about it.'' His eyes came back to Maya's. "It's a fascinating story, don't you agree Ms. Velaquez?''

The threat was obvious.

Maya held her breath until Patricia shook her head, a regretful frown on her face. "Nothing I'd like better, but at the moment, I can't. I have to deal with a *fieri facias*. We represent a CEO who's on the hot seat right now, and I need to return to his problems.'' She looked back at Maya. "That's why I'm here, bothering you in the first place. You wouldn't have the Andrews file, would you?''

"It's on my secretary's desk, waiting to be filed.'' Seeing a way out, Maya took a step forward. "I'll go get it for you—''

"No, no…'' Patricia held up her hand and cut off Maya's escape. "I can find it. You two go get your coffee, but keep me updated, Maya. Your case sounds much more interesting.'' Shaking Shepard's hand once more, she nodded to Maya and left.

Shepard inclined his head toward the hallway, his dark eyes steady and unperturbed as he held out his hand, the one still holding the umbrella. It dripped silently on the rug.

''Shall we go?'' he asked. ''I have a rental car out front.''

Maya felt her stomach clench at the way he'd manipulated her, but considering the choices—and his less than subtle threat—leaving the office was probably safer, at least for her reputation.

''I'll take my car and you take yours,'' she said tightly. ''I drive a white Volvo. When you see me pull out of the parking lot, you can follow.''

Brushing past him, she headed down the hall without waiting to hear his reply.

SHE'D KNOWN he wasn't Renaldo.

Renaldo was dead.

But it'd taken her heart a moment longer than her brain to remember that fact. When she'd looked up and seen Shepard Reyes in the doorway, the past had rushed in with him. He had the same smoldering look, the same glittering eyes, the same arrogant air of the man who'd become her lover when she'd been fifteen.

Her life before she came to the States seemed to

have happened to another person. In fact, it came to her almost as a movie, the scenes something she felt she'd witnessed, instead of experienced.

Driving toward Montrose with Shepard Reyes behind her, Maya let the memories flood her, the difference between the two brothers coming into sharp relief.

Renaldo had been twenty-two when he died so Shepard had to be forty-five. Renaldo had been sleek and quick, a shadow who had lived in the darkness. Shepard seemed just the opposite—his presence couldn't be ignored. He was taller and heavier than Renaldo would have ever been, his shoulders broad beneath his expensive suit, his black eyes more focused.

And he was, Maya suspected all at once, much, much more dangerous.

She took a deep breath and let it out slowly. She could handle this man and his threats, she told herself. Shepard Reyes and all he represented meant nothing to her and she'd be silly to let him rattle her. His demands had frightened her but they were meaningless—as long as he wanted something from her, which he clearly did.

Which brought her to the next question.

Just what in the hell *did* he want?

She exited the freeway and turned right, going beneath the underpass. In any other section of Houston, the streets would have been full of commuters heading to work but not here. The off-beat haven of the artistic and gay communities, Montrose never shut down. Slowing as she reached the main commercial area, Maya passed a tattoo place with three people already in the chairs, a group of twenty-somethings spilling out of the latest trendy diner and a beautifully decorated pocket park, maintained, a sign on the sidewalk said, by the Houston Gay Men's Choir. After a moment, she spotted her destination, directly across from the park.

She'd been to the outre coffee shop a few months before to meet a blind date. The guy had been a disaster, but she'd liked the place, probably because it wasn't the kind of restaurant she normally visited...which was exactly why she'd come here now. Most of the lawyers she knew would abandon their Beemers in the middle of Interstate 10 before they'd be caught in the Jumped-Up Java Bar. She parked then climbed from her car and locked it. Her eyes went to the townhouses under construction across the street. Despite its eccentricity, the area was growing. To buy a home in Montrose, you needed a fortune.

But a very small one...compared to that of the Reyes clan.

They owned half of Colombia, the half that held the emerald mines, and their power was unquestionable. Renaldo had turned away from a future filled with ease and luxury when he'd taken up *la causa*. He'd been foolish, of course. If he'd wanted a better life for those less fortunate, he should have worked with the wealth of his family to bring that about. But he'd been too young and foolish to see that.

And she'd been too young and in love to see beyond him.

Shepard Reyes pulled his rental car into the empty spot where she waited, their eyes meeting through the windshield. A sinking sensation assaulted her; the past was about to catch up with her.

SHEPARD REYES WAS a bastard, but he didn't care.

He'd come to Houston for answers and he was prepared to do whatever it took to get them.

Following Maya to a small café, he held open the door and they went in, Maya leading him to a table in the very back. They gave their orders to a young girl who sported three eyebrow rings and a snake tattoo on her neck.

Just as she stepped away from their table, the bell above the front door rang loudly. Maya's gaze shot over Shepard's shoulder and he took the moment to study her without her knowledge. She wore a business suit the color of café au lait and a dark silk blouse beneath it. The fabric shimmered in the harsh overhead lights but not as much as her hair. The thick, shining mass was pulled into a severe bun, and he suspected she wanted to disguise its beauty for some reason.

The thought was ridiculous, he told himself, but the fact that he had it in the first place was even more outrageous. Why did he care? Shifting in his seat, he followed Maya's stare, taking in the two people who'd entered. They were dressed in the same nondescript clothing their server wore and seemed to favor the same body jewelry. One had pink hair and the other had blue.

Shepard turned back to the woman across the table from him. "Is this where all the important attorneys in Houston come for coffee?"

Unamused, she stared at him with a sudden and heated directness, her answer as obvious as his question. "I brought you here so no one I care about would see us. I don't know what you want, Mr. Reyes, but I'd just as soon we do this fast—"

"*Por favor,* call me Shepard."

She put her elbows on the table and leaned toward him. Anyone seeing them might think they were lovers reluctant to part, sharing one last intimate moment before leaving reluctantly.

But that image only worked if their conversation was not overheard.

"I don't want to call you anything," she answered, her voice tight with undisguised anger. "I don't want to be here and I don't want to talk to you. The only reason I agreed to this—'' she waved her hand to the tables around them ''—was to get you out of my office.''

Shepard looked into her eyes as she spoke and all at once, he was struck by a realization; Maya Vega was a very complex—and contradictory—woman. Beneath the cool exterior, there was heat. Beneath the sophistication, there was doubt. Beneath the beauty, there was pain. The wall she'd built around her true emotions was thick and sturdy, and it'd obviously been in place for years. No one, especially him, could ever get around it.

Shepard wasn't a man who had insights and the unexpected revelation surprised him. But he knew it was right. ''I understand,'' he said quietly. ''But—''

''No, you don't,'' she interrupted. ''You don't understand and you don't care or you wouldn't be here.'' Her lips compressed into a narrow line, as if she were trying to hold in her words but couldn't. ''Just tell me what you want, then get the hell out of my life.''

His coffee arrived before Shepard could answer. He pulled his steaming mug toward him but Maya ignored the tea she'd ordered.

''I will do exactly that,'' he replied. ''As soon as you answer my questions.''

''All right.'' Her voice was not as steady as it had

been in her office. "But tell me first, how did you find me?"

"The Reyes family has many friends here in the States." He added sugar to his coffee and stirred slowly, lifting his gaze to hers. "They were happy to help me when I told them I was trying to locate you."

She took a second to absorb the implication, then filed it away for further study. Truth be told, she probably used the same investigators he'd hired. They were the best in town and even the fact that she'd changed her last name would have meant nothing to them.

"And why did you need to locate me?"

"As I said earlier, I've been given some information that I need to confirm. No one but you can do that for me. It involves my brother…and you."

"There's nothing there to confirm or deny. What happened between the two of us took place too many years ago to matter now. You've come a long way on a fool's errand."

"You don't want to revisit your past?"

"Not the one you know," she said.

"You have another one? One I don't know about?"

Her eyes were so dark he had the sudden thought that he wouldn't be able to read them if the lights were dim and they were in bed.

Her answer stopped him from taking the image any further. ''You're clearly aware that no one here knows anything about…my younger years. For obvious reasons, I want to keep it that way.''

''Because of your career?''

''Partially,'' she admitted.

''But also because…''

''But also because it's painful for me.'' Her fingers rested lightly on the tabletop. They were tipped in pale polish and perfectly manicured. ''I prefer to focus on the present and my work. Nothing else is relevant. My friends have accepted the facts for what they are. They know that I came to the U.S. from South America following the death of my parents. That I was young. That I made it on my own with the help of some good people. That's it.'' She paused. ''And while we're being so frank, I'll take the opportunity to correct you, as well. I was not a leftist guerrilla. I did not share your brother's politics.''

''I find that hard to believe.''

She shrugged. ''That's your problem, not mine.''

''Are you sure about that?''

She threaded her fingers together but she gave no other sign of nervousness, answering his question with one of her own. ''Why are you here, Mr. Reyes? What is it you really want from me?''

''I want the truth.''

"Why?"

"It serves itself. That's the reward."

"You're too smart to believe platitudes." Her voice was blunt, her expression cynical. "You grew up in Colombia. There is no *one* truth, especially there. Surely you know that."

"Perhaps…" He moved to the edge of his chair and leaned closer to her, his words so softly spoken no one else could possibly hear them. "All I care about is the truth that concerns *mi familia.* And you understand that truth, as well. You were part of it."

"I don't know what you're talking about."

"Yes, you do," he said. "When you were a teenager, you took a lover five years your senior. He was my brother but he was also a criminal who killed and stole then justified his actions in the name of a revolution. And you were right there with him, every step of the way. In the end, he paid for his foolishness with his life."

"He made his own choices," she said stubbornly.

"And so did you. But there's more to the story than just that, isn't there?" He didn't wait for her answer. "A woman recently came into my office. For reasons that are not important, she told me something. It was a secret, she said. I think now she gave this information to me as much to relieve her own guilt as for anything else."

Maya Vega's face slowly became the color of bones.

"You know what she told me, don't you?"

"Of course not. How could I?" She licked her lips. "Who was this woman?"

"She claimed to be your *tía*." He stared at her closely. "Did you have an aunt?"

"Yes, I did," she admitted. "But she's probably dead by now. She lived a very hard life and I doubt it was a long one. I can't imagine why she would come to you with any kind of secret."

"You have no idea?"

"None whatsoever." She looked him straight in the eye.

"You're lying."

Her hand went to her throat and the gold cross that lay in the hollow of her neck. The chain that held it glistened in the light from the windows behind Shepard.

"Now is the time for the truth to come out." He leaned closer still. "Tell me, Maya Vega. Did you have my brother's child?"

MAYA STIFFENED at Shepard's question, ice-cold fear suddenly barring an escape. She wasn't sure, but she thought her heart might have stopped, as well. There seemed to be no blood flowing in her veins, no oxygen going to her brain.

Then he softly spoke. "Maya?"

Hearing her name broke her paralysis. She stood abruptly, her leg hitting the edge of the table so hard it rocked violently and threatened to tip over. As Shepard's mug did just that and his coffee spilled, he grabbed the table.

Maya was across the street and heading for the park before Shepard caught up with her.

HE REACHED HER SIDE and put his hand on her arm, pulling her around to face him. In another time and place she would have protested the touch, but it hardly seemed important at this juncture. His grip was strong and unequivocal. She looked down at his fingers, and then up, into his eyes. "Go away," she said. "Leave me alone."

"I can't do that. Not until you tell me the truth."

"I could call the police, Mr. Reyes. In case you don't know, things work differently in the States. Your name means nothing here. The authorities would be happy to help me."

"I'm sure they would," he said quietly. "As happy as the press would be to hear the reason I came to you in the first place."

"No doubt you're right, but there are other avenues I could take. I have friends, too. And I don't think they would appreciate your harassment of me."

"Are they the ones who will help you become a judge? If they are, you'd best watch them yourself. Friends like that flee when they find out they've been lied to."

"I've lied to no one."

"Your lies are lies of omission. You've built your reputation on strong ethics and a solid stance. You are known for being a woman who always does the right thing, the proper thing. If your supporters knew you'd been hiding a violent past, how do you think they'd feel?"

"What do you want from me, Mr. Reyes?"

His black eyes pinned her. "I want the truth." He paused. "Did you have my brother's child or not?"

His gaze held her fast, forcing her to realize she had no way out. She had to comply…or lose everything she'd worked for—which was probably going to happen regardless, she realized with a sinking heart. "Yes," she said finally. "I did."

Something flickered across his face—surprise or disbelief, she couldn't tell which—then he dropped her arm and went to a nearby bench to stand motionless, his hand gripping the back of it as if he needed the support. Ironically, the sun had come out and chased away the clouds. It was cool and quiet as she came to where he stood.

They stayed that way, still and silent, until he turned to her. She immediately lifted a hand to stave off his questions. "I'll tell you everything," she said, "but I want something in return."

"What?"

"I want you to leave me alone. I never want to see you or anyone in your family near me ever again."

He inclined his head slightly. "If that is what you want, you have my promise."

She wasn't sure why, but she believed him. She sat down abruptly and her heart tightened, preparing her for the fresh pain she knew her words would bring.

"The child died." She looked across the park at a bed of antique roses. Strangely enough, one held a single bloom. "At birth. I almost followed."

Shepard's features shifted into an expression Maya couldn't read. "When did this happen?"

"The day he was born—the same day Renaldo was captured."

"You lived with your aunt…and uncle, right?"

"Until they threw me out of their house the day I gave birth." Remembering Renita's fierce fight with Segundo, Maya felt ill, the angry words and sounds as penetrating now as they had been then, piercing her consciousness with fresh pain. She closed her eyes, unable to imagine what circumstance could have forced Renita to come to the Reyes family with her secrets. Praying her aunt was all right, Maya opened her eyes when she felt movement beside her. Shepard had sat down.

"They were unhappy with you for being pregnant?"

"My uncle was, but in reality I *had* to leave. It would have been dangerous for them if I had stayed. As long as Renaldo was there, the regular Colombian Army left the family alone. The soldiers were scared of him and the rebel cadre he commanded. But he'd already gone into hiding when my labor started. Rumors of his pending capture had been circulating and he'd been worried."

Shepard frowned as she spoke, but he didn't interrupt her and she continued.

"With Renaldo gone, Segundo and I both knew the whole family might be killed, either by FARC or the Army, the first because I knew too much and the latter because they could... My uncle was a cruel and stupid man, but at the same time he understood how things worked."

"You didn't care for him?"

She hesitated. "He wasn't a good person."

Falling silent, Shepard seemed to consider her answer. After a bit, he spoke again, his unexpected words a bombshell in the stillness of the park. "Your aunt told me that your child survived."

Maya jerked her head up, her breath catching in her throat. "What?"

"She said the child didn't die."

"No, that's not true." Maya shook her head. "I—I don't know why she would lie about that."

"Are you sure it's me she is lying to? You were young, you were scared, you had to have been in pain. You could have been confused…"

"The baby *died.*"

"You are positive?"

Her throat ached but she'd choke before she'd let him see her cry. She waited until she could control herself, then she answered. "You came for the truth and that's what I'm giving you. I have nothing to hide because you know it all." She drew a breath then let it out slowly. "The child died, Mr. Reyes. Believe me… I saw the body and there was no life left in it. That baby did not survive."

THE BREAK IN HER COMPOSURE affected Shepard unexpectedly. He raised a finger to her face and drew a line down her cheek with the back of one knuckle. Her skin was the color of marble but it felt like velvet, warm and soft. She didn't move and he dropped his hand, the whole incident over so quickly, he wondered for a second if he'd lost his mind and actually touched her or just thought about it.

"Are you absolutely certain?" he asked once more. "It's very important."

"I've never been more sure of anything in my life."

"All right then," he said quietly. "I will leave." He stood up and started down the sidewalk. But two steps away from Maya, he stopped and turned. She hadn't moved and for some reason, Shepard knew he would never forget the sight of her sitting there in the pale winter sun.

"I'm sorry." The words slipped out before he could stop them.

She lifted her gaze, the rest of her as still as a statue. "It was for the best." Her words had the hollow ring of something she'd told herself many times but had yet to believe.

"I'm not talking about your loss."

She waited.

"I'm sorry you loved my brother," he said. "He wasn't worth what it cost you...but I guess you know that by now."

WITH NO REASON TO STAY longer, Shepard went straight to the airport. He'd gotten what he'd come for. He wasn't shocked or even surprised by Maya Vega's admission of having the child, but he felt she had told him the truth.

If she'd lied, however, then it was just a matter of time. Others would learn what Shepard had and Maya's son would be discovered. Then killed. If that happened, Shepard would have the blood of his nephew on his hands unless he did something to protect him.

His cell phone rang as he entered the airport terminal.

"Sí."

Eduard Reyes's voice wasn't the stern one of Shepard's youth, but his father's haughty demeanor belied his age. He wasted no chitchat on his son. "When are you returning?" he demanded. "Javier has a problem and we need you here."

Shepard paused by one of the huge windows that looked out toward the runways. They stretched for miles, it seemed, their expansion restricted by a ring of industrial hangars. His father's bed faced the Andes, and Shepard wished he were staring at those mountains instead.

"I'm at the airport now. I'll be on the next flight out. What's the problem?"

His father ignored his question. "Did you attend to your foolishness?"

He'd told his family he was thinking of opening a second retail outlet in Houston. The excuse had seemed reasonable to him because they had a small shop in Bogota already. Its profits were huge, but so were the hassles. No one had been pleased by his idea but they would have been even more upset had he told them the truth of his mission. Especially Javier.

"Yes, I did." Shepard lied, but followed it with the truth. "I'm not sure what my next step will be."

"I suggest you come home and tend to your real business before the mines fall in and I must rescue everyone myself. I'm not too old, you know. I could go back to work tomorrow."

"That's not necessary, Papá. And besides, you know the doctors—"

"Los doctores pueden ir al infierno."

"Yes, well, I'm sure they need doctors in Hell, but you need them more." Shepard shook his head. "Tell Javier I'll be home as soon as I can." He started to say more, then he realized he was talking to an empty line. His father had hung up.

Shepard muttered a curse, then continued down the hallway toward his gate, the added worry of what Javier's problem might be now accompanying him. Every time Shepard left, Javier would call their father and inform him of some catastrophe. Before Shepard could return, however, Javier always "handled" the mysterious problem, earning for himself, as always, more credit than was ever due.

It'd been his technique for years.

Renaldo had been the baby of the family, and he'd always been indulged. Luisa, the boys' sister, did nothing right. Shepard, the middle son, cleaned up after everyone.

After Renaldo's death, however, Javier had claimed the spot of favorite and how he'd chosen to do so was simple.

He'd killed his way to the top.

CHAPTER THREE

THE SOUND OF a crying child woke her.

Maya sat straight up in the bed and pushed the hair from her eyes, her hands trembling, her heart beating crazily. A second passed—and then another—before she realized she'd been dreaming. There was no child.

She swallowed with effort, her throat dry and scratchy. Rising from the bed, she walked into her bathroom and turned on the faucet, sticking her cupped hands beneath the flow then bringing them to her mouth. She drank deeply, but the icy water made her feel worse. Lifting her gaze to the mirror, she saw a lost woman with empty eyes and tangled hair staring back. Maya moaned and dropped her head again, her hands resting on either side of the sink.

Shepard Reyes's presence had bullied its way inside her defenses and was holding her hostage. Four days had passed since he'd been there but not an hour had gone by without her thinking of what he'd said. The implication was almost too much to consider yet she'd done nothing but obsess over his supposed news.

Maya headed back toward her bed but as she sat down on the edge of the mattress, she wondered what she was doing. Why bother? She wouldn't go to sleep, no matter how hard she tried—she knew because she'd woken up every night since he'd left and the results had been the same.

She was so exhausted, she'd actually called in early that morning and told Darlene she'd be working from home. Most of the attorneys put in at least half a day on Saturday; Maya usually stayed the whole day. After lying to her secretary, Maya had fallen into bed, a restless imitation of slumber overtaking her until she'd had the dream.

The phone rang suddenly and interrupted her gloomy thoughts. She wasn't surprised it was Patricia.

"Maya? Darlene told me you weren't coming in today. Is everything okay?"

Maya cursed the secretary and then herself. She should have just bucked up and gone to the office regardless.

"Absolutely," Maya said, standing up. "I'll probably come in this afternoon, but I wanted to be able to concentrate on my latest case. The phones and everything, you know…"

"Say no more," Patricia answered. "I understand completely. They drive me to distraction sometimes, too." She chuckled. "I should have known it was work but I was hoping something else might be keeping you at home."

Maya stopped at the edge of the bed, her foot halfway in her slipper, her heart rocketing. She immediately imagined the worst. Shepard had told her who he was. Shepard had told her about Maya's past. Shepard had... Maya forced her voice into calmness. "What kind of something else?"

Patricia's answer shocked Maya, but not as she'd anticipated.

"Well, let's just say that if I had a man in my office as good-looking as your co-counsel the other day, I'd hope to be going without some sleep. He was quite...striking."

Maya was glad Patricia couldn't see her expression. "Patricia, please... It's not what you think..."

"Don't be ridiculous, Maya. You're a grown woman. It's perfectly all right for you to have a suitor. In fact, someone like Shepard Reyes standing beside you on the podium would be a definite plus. He'd pull in more of the minority vote, plus he'd get every female with eyes in her head to the polls, hoping for a glimpse of him."

"I—I don't know what to say," she replied faintly.

"Don't say anything," Patricia answered. "Simply take care of yourself and have a good weekend." Her tone went playful. "Just don't work too hard with Mr. Reyes… I need you here on Monday with your focus intact. We've got to start on the Barfield case."

Chuckling once more, Patricia hung up.

Maya stood in shock for a second, then her feet moved of their own accord toward the kitchen. But her mind didn't. It stayed with the image Patricia's words had generated. Shepard Reyes *was* a handsome man, she supposed, if you went for that dark and dangerous kind of look. She'd made a studied effort to avoid men like that since she'd come to the States. Blond, blue eyes, clean-cut…those were the characteristics of the men she dated. When she dated.

No, Shepard Reyes didn't appeal at all to her. She'd be thrilled if she never laid eyes on him again.

Pushing any other possibility out of her mind, Maya started water boiling for tea. Maybe she should clean out some closets and take some things to Goodwill. There were boxes in her storage unit she needed to go through, too. And the rosebushes needed trimming. If she were going to stay home, she might as well be productive.

But by her third cup, she knew she wasn't going to do any of those things. Instead, she was going to do what she'd been doing ever since Shepard Reyes had walked into her office. She was going to think about him and her past. And about Renaldo. And about the baby…

She could still smell the smoke that had been in the air that morning. Drifting in through the open window, the scent had been so strong she'd gagged. No one but the richest in Punto Perdido had had propane to cook their meals. Everyone else, including her aunt and uncle, gathered firewood to fuel their stoves and heat their homes. The midwife who'd attended her, Amarilla, had been burning eucalyptus leaves, too. She'd said the pungent blue-gray smoke would purify the air so Maya could rest easier.

Torn apart by a pain she'd thought would never end, Maya had sunk into delirium, accompanied by the screaming voices of her aunt and uncle and all those stinging scents. Even now she couldn't stand to smell a fireplace.

She closed her eyes. After this many years, she would have thought her sorrow would have left her, but it'd been her steady companion through all her well-fought battles and her triumphs, too. Even in her brightest moments—her college graduation, passing the bar, the partnership at the firm—Maya hadn't been able to escape the memories. Over the past few years, she'd managed to contain them, but Shepard's appearance had given them new life.

Despite the pain, one fact remained the same. The child *had* died. The midwife had brought the body to the bed and held it close so Maya, too weak to even lift her arms, could see. Behind her shuttered eyes, she saw the baby again. The image of the tiny body, so still and colorless, had pressed itself into her brain. She'd never forget it.

Just like the trip that had followed. More than half sick and completely destitute, she'd slept in the jungle until she was strong enough to walk, stealing fruit from the market when no one was watching. A week later, she'd left the village on foot, faint and light-headed but determined. Two days after that, she'd joined a band of illegals. They'd made their way to the coast and then to Cartagena where they'd left by boat, sailing to a barren stretch of Mexico's eastern shore and landing at night somewhere between Tampico and Brownsville. The man who'd led them—their coyote—had been brutal; whatever his demands, everyone had complied, including Maya who'd nothing to pay for her passage except her youth and beauty.

Buried in the deepest, darkest shadows of her shame, she knew she'd done what she had to in order to survive, but the cost had been high. On some level, she really believed it was just as well the baby had died. A child couldn't have survived the nightmare trip.

Then she remembered. She'd barely been more than a child herself.

Maya stood up and went to the kitchen sink to dump her cold tea, her thoughts as black as the February storm clouds outside the window, her feelings as empty as her heart. Shepard's words echoed in the void.

Are you absolutely certain?

SHEPARD'S SUV SPED through the traffic of Bogota as he honked at the other cars and ignored the stop signs. A cacophony of noise assaulted his ears through the bulletproof glass, but that was all that could make it past the windows. His father had had the vehicle built ten years ago when trips to the mine had become too dangerous.

The roads were even more perilous now. Everyone knew that vehicles going *to* the mine held money while those *returning* carried emeralds. The chances of gaining something valuable were almost one hundred percent. For the most part, *las terroristas* left Shepard alone, the car simply an extra precaution. They knew they'd lose any fight with him— either on the spot or later, when they least expected it.

He pulled the armored vehicle into the driveway

of the Reyes family home and the security gate opened automatically, the guard stationed in the shack outside the brick fence watching for him. He parked quickly then crossed the tiled courtyard and strode through the front door into the entry. The cool, dim interior of the villa spoke of money and power but Shepard didn't notice.

He was still thinking about Maya Vega. He couldn't get over the fact that she was so different from the person he'd expected. Renaldo had drawn a mental picture for Shepard of a young girl, poor and hungry, who'd been swept away by Renaldo's brash bravado and promises of riches and escape. His cadre knew his true identity and of the fortune his family controlled. Maya had to have known, as well. To anyone in her situation, Renaldo would have been quite a prize.

Shepard had always assumed, as well, that she knew of her uncle's part in Renaldo's death.

But now he wasn't so sure. After talking to Maya, the situation—and the woman—seemed even more complicated than he'd thought.

Not only was she *not* the person he'd expected, she wasn't even the person she *pretended* to be. The protective wall he'd seen the day they'd met was a diversion. Maya was a total enigma, her real self hidden as deeply as the emeralds at Muzo. To make sure things stayed that way, she was working hard at fortifying that respectability: The black robe she wanted was more than a symbol of just how far she'd come—it would be a formidable shield against her past.

Unfortunately, however, her greatest weakness was that very past. And if he had breached it, others might, as well. The thought was ominous for one simple reason.

Eduard Reyes had never changed his will. The document read now as it had almost two decades before. The majority of the Muzo and all it represented was to go to his favorite son, Renaldo, and if not him, then to *his* heirs. Javier, Shepard and Luisa followed, in that order.

To Shepard, it had never mattered and he believed Luisa shared that sentiment. But Javier was a different story.

Shepard went up a floor, taking the steps two at a time, walking quickly to the door to his father's room. He knocked softly then entered.

His father looked as if he were already dead. Pale and thin, he lay beneath the sheets, his chest barely moving as he breathed. But his eyes fluttered open as Shepard came close and the illusion evaporated. The fire in their depths burned as brightly as always, if not more so.

"Did you talk to *El Idiota?*" he rasped.

Putting aside his worries about his brother, Shep-

ard sighed. "That's no way to refer to Colombia's
Minister of Mines, Papá. The man is—"

"The man is an idiot," his father reiterated.
"Anyone who wants to do the things he does has
no understanding of *los piedreros*. We've worked
with them for years." He feebly pounded his chest
with a gnarled fist. "The Reyes family knows the
miners better than they know themselves."

Eduard was right, but he was also wrong. For
years, the family had had free rein over how they
treated the workers, but times were changing. They
wanted a fair wage and good doctors and schools
for their children. Unlike everyone else in their family, Shepard agreed with the Minister of Mines who
thought the men deserved more.

"Have you picked out my casket?"

Eduard's question pulled Shepard from his
thoughts. He sat down in the chair next to the bed.
"No, I haven't," he answered. "Should I?"

"If you listen to that man and do what he says,
you'll kill me," Eduard replied. "You might as well
attend to the details."

Shepard's jaw tightened at Eduard's drama. His
father *was* a sick man—a sick seventy-year-old
man—but he'd attempted, without much success, to
manipulate Shepard for years. Thankfully, the door
to the bedroom opened before Shepard could
answer.

Shepard's mother and sister entered the room, the women moving toward the bed as if pulled by a string. An apt analogy, Shepard thought grimly. They were Eduard's puppets, controlled by love, hate or greed. That's why Eduard was always so frustrated with Shepard. He didn't play along.

Luisa, Shepard's sister, kissed her father's forehead then turned to Shepard. When she'd married twelve years ago, Eduard had purchased the home behind his own for her and she resided there with her son, Vincente, who was eleven, and her husband, Esteban.

"How was your trip?" she asked. "I'm sorry I haven't been over to see you but I've been busy."

As she spoke, she raised her hand and a brilliant flash of green pulled Shepard's gaze. He reached out and stilled her fingers. She had on a new ring—a marquise-shaped emerald surrounded by yellow diamonds. It was gaudy and unattractive but very flashy. Just Luisa's style.

"Do you like it?" Her fingers in his, she turned her hand to catch the sun beside Eduard's bed. "Esteban bought it for me last week."

Luisa's husband had worked in the mines almost as long as Shepard but in direct contrast to Shepard, Esteban did as little as possible while grabbing as much as he could. Shepard looked up at his sister, his expression frozen above the ring. "Did he pay for it or steal it?"

She snatched her hand from Shepard's grip. "He bought it," she said tightly. "You can check the manifests, if you doubt me."

"Don't be so mean to your *hermana*." In the soft, nonthreatening voice she always used, his mother, Marisol, scolded Shepard lightly. "She loves you."

"And I, her." Shepard gave his sister an apologetic smile. She caught the sharp end of Marisol's tongue as much as Shepard caught Eduard's. Shepard pitied her more than anything. "But Papá pays me to watch the mines. I'm merely being a good businessman."

With a frown, his sister moved past him to the other side of the bed, his mother returning her attention to her husband.

"How do you feel today?" she asked. "Did you drink your tea?"

Shepard glanced into the cup beside his father's bed. "Good God, Mother, what is that?"

"All Heal," she answered. "I've sprinkled it about the room, as well. It will help your father—"

"The only person that stinking mess helps is Teresa." Shepard grabbed the mug, then went to the window where he pitched out the pungent-smelling drink. Opening the bedroom door he placed the mug on a table in the corridor. "How much did you pay the witch for that disgusting stuff?"

His mother crossed herself. "She's not a witch. She's a *santera*. Don't speak of her like that."

Shepard hated the so-called "high priestess" his mother consulted. In his opinion all she did was relieve Marisol of cash and give nothing in return. Like many South Americans, however, Marisol liked to hedge her bets, keeping one foot in the traditional church, and the other with Santeria. Brought to the Americas with the slave trade, the religion was a complicated mixture of Catholic saints and African traditions, led by priests called santeros. All of them were well-versed in herbal remedies, which they claimed had power over everything from evil to insomnia.

Javier hadn't shared Shepard's feelings. In fact, he and the woman had been lovers at one time. As far as Shepard knew, they'd broken up years before but he had no idea why. In his mind, they deserved one another. An unholy alliance.

Shepard started to argue, but his father waved a weak hand, silencing them all. From the bed, his eyes drilled Shepard. "Let your mother have her silly herbs and your sister, her baubles. If you really want to do something to help me, then forget this ridiculous idea of opening a store and listen to your brother. He has a plan to get rid of that idiot minister. I want you to hear what he has to say."

Shepard could feel a muscle in his jaw twitch. Javier's strategies frequently lay outside the law, which was quite an accomplishment considering almost anything could—and did—happen in Colombia with no one caring one way or the other.

"That's right." A deep voice sounded behind them. "You should listen to your big brother, *hermanito*. He knows of what he speaks."

Marisol and Luisa greeted Javier with kisses but Shepard kept his seat.

Javier came to Shepard and slapped him on the back. They shared a faint family resemblance but little else. Where Shepard's weight was muscular and his face sharp, Javier's features had been blurred by the life he'd led, his body made soft by his indulgences.

"Was your trip to the States a good one?" His gaze was as steady as a hawk's watching prey. "Did you find what you sought?"

"I investigated the market," Shepard answered casually, "but I'm not sure retail is the way we want to go. You know how complicated it can be."

Javier nodded. A countless number of jewelry stores in Bogota sold emeralds but the small shop they had in the upscale area of Bogota was special, mainly because of who they were. Frequented by tourists, the tiny *bodega* made an incredible amount of money yet the hassles were equally huge. To open a long-distance endeavor would be daunting. Shepard had needed an excuse to go to Houston, though.

"I'm sure you will have something interesting to tell me, regardless of the outcome," Javier replied.

Shepard felt a flicker of unease then told himself he was being ridiculous. Javier couldn't possibly know anything about Maya Vega. Not at this point, anyway. On the other hand, Javier's doublespeak often covered up the truth. Shepard tilted his head slightly to indicate his agreement then made a mental note. He'd better check on Maya Vega…just to be sure.

He didn't need her blood on his hands, too.

MAYA HAD SWORN she'd never return to Colombia, but the words of Shepard Reyes continued to disturb her the following week. They burned their way through all logic and common sense and the longer she considered the possibility that her son might be alive, the more urgent it seemed that she investigate the situation personally. The idea in and of itself— that her one offspring could possibly be alive—was almost overwhelming but stepping past that impossible point, was another issue, this one almost as upsetting. She didn't trust any of the Reyeses. It was a huge leap to go from "Was he alive?" to the next question, but she'd made it quickly. If she was wrong and the boy had survived, what did Shepard want with him? Would he turn him into a Reyes? Teach him all their tricks?

She'd investigated the family after she'd left Colombia and become successful, and the report had confirmed all she'd witnessed in her earlier years. The family was ruthless when it came to dealing with their workers and even more so with their rivals. Power and profits meant more to them than anything else. Much, much more.

Renaldo had not been exempt from that attitude but she'd been too young and too innocent to realize it. Longing to impress him and ready to do anything for him, she'd listened as he'd complained constantly about a family who didn't understand him, who manipulated and controlled him...but he had done the very same thing to her. Through it all, though, she'd done the things she'd done because she'd loved *him*. Not his politics.

With Shepard's presence still vivid in her mind, she revisited that file, reading deep into the night.

Then she booked her flight.

Packing two nights before she was to leave, Maya continued to think long and hard about the choice she was making but her resolution stayed firm. The pending judgeship was of paramount importance, but there was no comparison between it and her son. If there was any possibility—no matter how remote—that he might be alive, she had to know. Any woman alive would feel the same.

Maya didn't believe in ESP but when her phone rang as she closed her suitcase, she knew exactly who was on the other end. She picked up the receiver with shaking fingers.

His voice sounded as if he were in the house next door. "*Señorita* Vega?"

She gripped the receiver with both hands. "I thought you weren't going to bother me anymore."

"I lied."

"And why is that?"

"I wanted to…make sure everything was all right with you."

His reply puzzled her until she looked down at her suitcase. Had he somehow found out she was going to Colombia? It didn't seem possible, but he'd mentioned friends who had helped him. Did these friends include someone who might be watching her? Was she being paranoid or cautious?

"Everything's just fine," she said slowly. "Why wouldn't it be?"

"No particular reason," he answered. "I merely wanted to make sure my visit had not troubled you too much. I appreciated your help. And I've come to think you might be right. Perhaps the woman I spoke to was lying. Who knows?''

His reversal was too smooth, too quick. Her suspicion took another leap when her doorbell rang. ''There's someone here—''

''I'll wait,'' he replied.

Torn between the fear she'd give herself away and the desire to see if he knew about her trip, she hesitated. ''All right,'' she finally agreed. ''But first let me see who's here.''

She hurried to her entry, still holding the phone as she looked through the sidelight to see a delivery man. She wasn't expecting anything, but Darlene could have sent something over. Everything was urgent to her secretary. Nervously scribbling her signature, Maya accepted the flat envelope he held and took it straight to her desk where she found her letter opener. The French pocketknife had been a gift from Patricia one Christmas, the hand-honed edge incredibly sharp.

Maya didn't even notice when the blade sliced into her palm.

Staring at the photograph she'd pulled from the envelope, she didn't realize she'd cut herself until blood splattered over the glossy paper. Nausea rolled over her. She grabbed a tissue from the box on the desk and stanched the bleeding, a sick emptiness suddenly filling her.

Shot from a distance with a telephoto lens, the edges of the picture were grainy and out of focus but the center was clear as could be.

It was a photograph of her. Taken nineteen years before, the picture showed her holding an automatic gun and surrounded by men equally armed. Renaldo was not in the frame because he'd been behind the camera. Thrusting his weapon into her hands, he'd pushed her into the group and told her to smile. She stared at the photograph and felt her heart careen out of control, sweat breaking out on her forehead as heavily as it had that day in the jungle.

She hadn't realized she'd said anything until she heard Shepard's voice, coming from the phone she'd set down on the desk. "Maya? Maya? Are you still there? Hello?"

His voice triggered something and suddenly she understood. She grabbed the receiver.

"What in the hell do you think you're doing?" Her voice was ferocious. "I tried to help you and this is the thanks I get?"

"What are you talking about?"

"Don't play the innocent with me. I'm holding a photograph and you damn well know what it is. That's why you called, isn't it? Your timing was perfect but you can take your little warning and shove it up your—"

"I have no idea what you're talking about. Explain yourself."

His command was so forceful, Maya complied without thinking. "I just received a photograph of me," she said tightly. "With Renaldo's cadre." Her voice went hoarse. "It won't work, Shepard."

She thought she heard a quick intake of breath, then knew she'd imagined it. "I have sent you nothing. This photograph must have come from someone else—"

"Say something I can believe."

"I am telling you the truth."

Anger washed over her. "If you think this will deter me, think again. You and your family can try all the dirty tricks you have at your disposal but they won't work against me. Or my son, if he lives."

She didn't realize she was speaking Spanish until she stopped. And she didn't realize how much she meant her words until then, either. Compared to the possibility her son might be alive, nothing else in her life mattered. Nothing.

She spoke again. "Are we clear on this? I am coming to Colombia and there is nothing you can do about it."

"That is not a good idea." He sounded alarmed but she knew he was faking it. "Please, Maya. Do not even consider coming here."

Maya looked down at the photo in her hand. She'd smeared blood on it, darkening the edges and causing them to curl. "Your plan has backfired, *Señor* Reyes. Nothing could stop me now."

CHAPTER FOUR

"HOW LONG WILL you be gone?" Patricia's voice held more than a hint of disappointment when Maya stopped by her office the following morning.

"I'm not sure," Maya hedged. "But I have too much going on here to be away long."

Patricia's fingers tapped the top of her desk. "Next Saturday night is the dinner for Senator Hayes. I wanted to introduce you to some people there."

"I know, Patricia." Maya shook her head. "I'd planned on attending but this came up and I don't have a choice now. I have to deal with the situation. They're asking for me."

"This is the Sanchez case?"

Maya had resorted once again to the lie she'd told when she'd introduced Shepard to Patricia. She'd researched the case last night just to make sure she had the facts straight. "Yes, it is. We did the probate in '97. I think you might have been in Switzerland at the time."

Patricia frowned as she tried to remember but Maya rushed into her explanation. She didn't want Patricia thinking about the case too hard.

"Sr. Reyes has located the missing son who left right after the Sanchez funeral. Obviously they haven't been able to close the estate without him so now that he's been found, the family wants me to fly to Bogota and wrap things up."

"Well, it can't be avoided, I suppose, but make sure you don't get in too deep." Patricia nodded then reached for a folder on her desk, looking at Maya over her glasses. "You really need to be back by the end of next week. The governor might come into town and if he does, we'll want you in front of him."

Backing out of the office, Maya clutched the file and made a promise she didn't know if she could keep. "Of course. I'll be back by then." She'd made it to the threshold when Patricia spoke again.

"Maya?"

She stopped and so did her heart. "Yes?"

"If this trip was personal, it'd be fine, you know. You're an adult and you have a right to your private life."

A flood of guilt hit Maya as she understood. Patricia thought she was going to meet Shepard for a romantic tryst. "I know that, Patricia. And I would tell you if that was the case.'' She paused. ''But it's not what you think.''

She fled, leaving her lie behind her.

The Avianca flight left Bush International the following morning at 6:30 a.m. Maya settled into her first-class seat and tried to stay composed. The plane would arrive in Miami around ten. She'd have a layover until one at which point she'd then board another 757. By 3:30 that afternoon, she'd be in Bogota.

Turning down the flight attendant's offerings, Maya retrieved a report she'd brought and tried to read it. The airplane hadn't even gotten off the ground before she gave up. Her brain was spinning as fast as the jet's engines—there was no way she could concentrate.

They banked sharply and her papers slid across her lap. Maya grabbed them, the task jarring her and forcing her once more to question her sanity.

If her son had survived, she wanted to know—*had to know*—but something told her she might come to regret this trip…a thousand times over.

SHEPARD WAS SITTING on the patio having his morning coffee when his mother walked outside. Normally she wasn't up this early and he should have been surprised to see her but he was too busy worrying about Maya to notice anything else. She had no idea what she was doing, no idea of the peril that faced her here. If Colombia had been dangerous to her before, it might be deadly this time. He wasn't sure he could protect her and he didn't know why he even cared.

But he did.

"May I join you?"

His mother's soft request brought Shepard's gaze up. He rose to his feet and pulled out her chair. "Of course. Please…" She sat down and one of the maids appeared, a tray in hand with Marisol's herbal tea and two pieces of *pan dulce*. Shepard reclaimed his chair as Marisol reached for one of the sweet rolls. Instead of eating the bread, however, she crumbled it absentmindedly, her thoughts clearly troubled.

"Your sister is very upset," she said after a while. "She thinks you are making a grave mistake with this idea of another store, especially one so far away."

"Luisa doesn't approve of anything I do." Shepard shrugged. "I'm not surprised she's unhappy."

"She's protecting her husband. She thinks Esteban should have more responsibility and authority with the company and she knows you would run the new shop."

Shepard took a sip of his coffee and considered his mother's comment. The information itself wasn't important; what mattered was the fact she'd brought it up at all. Marisol, more than any of them, did Eduard's bidding without exception. If she were using her daughter to deliver a message from Eduard it wouldn't be the first time. But then Shepard reconsidered. He'd already heard his father's opinion on this topic. Perhaps it was Marisol herself who was upset with the turn of events.

"Esteban's doing as much as he wants to—and he couldn't handle more authority." Shepard put down his coffee, the cup hitting the saucer with a clink that mixed with the call of the macaws in the aviary behind the garden.

Marisol made no comment. They sat in silence then she tore off another piece of bread and spoke. By the tone of her voice, Shepard immediately knew her remarks about the store were not what had brought her to him.

"Do you ever think of Renaldo?"

Her question caught him off guard. His mother hadn't mentioned her youngest son's name in years. Why did she bring him up now of all times?

"Why do you ask me that, Mama?"

"¿Por qué?" She pursed her lips and touched the crucifix she wore. "He has been on my mind lately. Teresa says…"

Shepard almost interrupted her but for some unaccountable reason, he urged his mother on. "Teresa says?"

"Teresa says his spirit has been trying to contact her. She says he's disturbed about some things that are going on right now."

Despite his interest, Shepard's distrust of the santera was too ingrained to consider the timing anything but coincidental. He teased his mother gently, trying to make her see how ridiculous the idea was. "Mama, please...do you really believe Renaldo is speaking from his grave? If he had something important to say, why would he use Teresa? He'd go straight to you."

His mother's expression immediately shifted, a sternness he'd rarely seen coming over her features. "You mock me."

"It's not you I mock, Mama. I simply don't believe Teresa can take messages from the dead."

Her eyes held his a moment longer, then she stood, her back as straight as iron, her gaze just as flinty.

"If you choose not to believe, that is your decision. But it wasn't me she said Renaldo wanted to contact." Her jaw went tight. "It was you."

MAYA HAD HER MASK IN PLACE by the time the plane landed at El Dorado International Airport.

Anyone who looked at her would be totally ignorant of the fear and anxiety inside her heart.

But she knew. Everything she'd tried to hide for years was about to be exposed and she was scared to death.

Walking out of the jetway and into the terminal, she told herself she'd faced worse situations and had come through them all right. She'd do the same with this. If her son was still alive—a fact she doubted highly—then she'd find him. If he hadn't survived, she'd face the grief once more and then go on with her life.

Maya's eyes skipped over the jumble of people waiting at the gate. She'd expected Shepard to send someone to the airport to watch for her. If he had done so, however, he'd be sorely disappointed. They'd had excellent tail winds and the flight had come in quite early. No one approached her even after she went through the necessary procedures and picked up her bag. Shouldering her way through the crowd, Maya made her way outside where she took the first taxi in line.

The ancient vehicle left the terminal and quickly sped toward town. The airport was twelve kilometers east of the city's main section, but her destination was on the outskirts of Bogota. All Maya could do was stare out the window, her stomach churning. She'd been to the city once as a child and had been overwhelmed. The noise and traffic and people had merged into one giant mass of terror. She felt the same way now but for a much different reason—the teeming streets and endless vehicles meant nothing compared to the man she knew she'd soon see.

The trip to the other side of town seemed to go on forever, but when the driver slowed and pulled into a guarded entry, Maya wished it'd taken longer. Through the lacy ironwork blocking their way, she could see the villa and surrounding grounds. The setting was more impressive than she'd been prepared for—the sprawling, multi-winged house and tiled roof were typical in architecture for the area but very untypical in scale.

She was staring and wondering just what the hell she thought she was doing when she realized the taxi driver and the guard were having a heated exchange.

She leaned forward over the front seat. "What's the problem?"

"He won't let us in." The driver jerked a thumb toward the guard then muttered a curse beneath his breath. That everyone could hear.

Maya opened her window and spoke in an imperative way, her chin up, her look full of disdain. "I'm a friend of *Señor* Reyes. He's going to be very unhappy when he hears of your misconduct. If you do your job and let us in without further grief, I'll see that he doesn't know. But if you continue to persist..." Arching one eyebrow, she let her voice die out, the implication clear.

The man wanted to refuse, but he wanted his job, as well. Finally, he punched the button for the gate and it swung back slowly. Maya nodded and rolled up her window, her expression changing the minute the guard could no longer see her. Ashamed at the way she'd bullied the man, she wondered how long she'd have to be gone before she'd forget how things were done in Colombia.

The car stopped and more nervous than ever, Maya paid the driver then slipped from the vehicle. With a determination she didn't really feel, she walked quickly up a sidewalk lined with swaying red hibiscus blooms and rang the bell.

CHAPTER FIVE

AN ETERNITY PASSED. Then a woman opened the door. Strikingly handsome, she was dressed entirely in white, her silvery hair hanging almost to her waist, her green eyes glowing with curiosity. Maya couldn't even begin to guess her age. "*¿Sí?*"

Maya's well-thought-out plan suddenly seemed silly and inadequate for the task. "Is...is the *Señora* Reyes home?"

"*Sí.*" The woman answered with a smile, her curious eyes sweeping over Maya.

"I'd like to see her, please. I'm...an acquaintance of Shepard's."

"Of course, please come in." She stepped out of the way, then waved toward a sitting room at her left as she closed the door behind Maya. Her perfume filled the air between them, an unfamiliar scent, strong but not unpleasant. "You should have told me you wanted him. Please go in and sit down, and I'll see if he's back—"

"No, no." Maya saw her scheme dying before it

even had a chance. "I'm not here to see Shepard. I wanted to talk to his mother. He's at the mine to-day…isn't he?"

Halfway out of the room, the woman paused with a puzzled look. "He left early this morning for Muzo, yes." She stared at Maya and seemed to weigh her options. After a moment she nodded, something apparently satisfying her. "All right. Wait here. I'll go get *Señora* Reyes."

She glided out of the room, and Maya sank down to one of the three sofas that filled the generous space, apprehension bombarding her. What was she doing? What was she going to find out by coming here? Was she crazy?

The woman was gone long enough for Maya to decide she *was* crazy, then she returned, a shorter, stouter woman walking slowly beside her. Maya stood as the older one came forward.

Her voice held the authority of her position and class, a fact of which Maya could tell she was clearly well aware. "I am Marisol Reyes. I understand you're a friend of my son's?"

"We're…associates." Maya held out her hand. "I'm Maya Velaquez."

Shepard's mother took Maya's fingers in her own then let them go, raising her hand behind her, to indicate the woman at the back of the room. "This is my friend, Teresa Montoya."

Maya smiled at the woman by the doorway. Something about her was unsettling yet at the same time, intriguing. She would have made the perfect attorney, Maya decided. *"Mucho gusto, Señora."*

The woman acknowledged Maya with a nod, but Shepard's mother was already speaking again, her eyes on Maya. "Some coffee would be nice, Teresa. Would you please tell the kitchen to bring us some?"

The woman left without a sound, her peculiar perfume going with her. Marisol Reyes looked at Maya and she knew the time had come.

"Teresa told me you wanted to talk to me..."

As Maya started to speak her heart dropped, trapping her breath inside her chest as surely as she was trapped in the room.

A second later, Shepard emerged from the shadows.

HE WASN'T THAT SHOCKED to see Maya, but her appearance still hit Shepard hard. He ignored his reaction and approached her, speaking as if he were glad to see her.

"Maya Velaquez! Why didn't you tell me you were coming?" He crossed the room and swept Maya into a hug, kissing her on both cheeks. She stood stiffly in the circle of his embrace, then seemed to realize she needed to reciprocate. Her arms went around his waist and she patted his back, the swell of her breasts brushing his chest. Looking down at her, he held her so she couldn't move. Her eyes flashed daggers at him. "You should have let me know you were arriving today and I would have picked you up at the airport."

She moved out of his arms with a subtle twist. "I wasn't sure what time the plane would actually land."

"I see you've met my mother."

"Yes, I have. And *Señora* Montoya, as well." She tilted her head toward Teresa who entered the room with a tray of coffee things.

"Then I got here just in time, didn't I?"

Marisol's voice was polite but Shepard heard the hint of suspicion behind her words. "Why haven't I met your friend before now, Shepard? Where have you been hiding this lovely lady?"

Maya answered quickly. "I live in Houston, *Señora*. I'm an attorney and this isn't what you're thinking—"

Shepard held up a hand and cut off her words, a parody of the scene they'd played out in her office unfolding once more. "Let me explain," he commanded.

Maya's gaze burned but she held out a hand as if to tell him to proceed.

"Maya is the attorney who represents the retail

jewelry store I looked into buying in Houston last month. I invited her to come down and see the mines but I didn't think she was going to take me up on the offer.'' He turned from his mother to look at Maya again. ''I'm certainly glad you made it.''

''I couldn't stay away,'' Maya replied. ''The situation is much too important for me to ignore. I made reservations at the Hotel Parque as soon as I could after we met.''

''Oh, no,'' Marisol said. ''We can't have that.'' Her reserve continued but she did what any proper Latin would do; she offered her hospitality. ''We have plenty of room here. You must stay with us.''

Maya smiled sweetly at Shepard's mother and even though it wasn't a genuine expression, Shepard found himself transfixed. For one fleeting second, he caught a glance of another woman, someone she might have been a long time ago.

''I can't do that. Your generosity is too much, Señora. I couldn't possibly impose on you to such a degree.''

''Nonsense,'' Marisol replied. ''It would be an imposition on us if you turn down the offer. I insist.''

With dark eyes full of helplessness, Maya looked in Shepard's direction. He considered giving her a way out, then he thought again. There was no better way to keep an eye on her than to have her under his roof. And if she did indeed find her son, Shepard would be the first to know.

"She's right," Shepard said, tilting his head toward his mother. "You need to stay here since we'll be working so closely together. Going back and forth to the office and then out to the mine…we'd waste all our time in traffic. Besides that, I'm sure the rest of the family will want to meet you. The mine is everyone's business."

Turning back to Marisol, Maya smiled tightly. "Well, it seems I have no choice, *Señora*—I guess I'll have to stay right here."

MARISOL AND TERESA DEPARTED to arrange for the preparation of Maya's room, leaving Maya alone with the man who wanted to ruin her life.

She looked at Shepard, her body still humming from the unexpected physical contact with him. She didn't want to consider what her reaction meant. "I'm not sure what you think you're doing, but if that was your idea of intimidation, I can do without it."

"What would you have liked me to do, Maya? Tell my mother the truth?" He shook his head, a dark lock of hair falling over his left brow. "That would not be a good idea, believe me."

"I had no intention of telling her who I was. Or of telling anyone."

"Then what were you going to do? Why are you here?"

"I'm an attorney," she said calmly. "I do investigations for estates all the time. It's easy to get people to talk to you when they think you have money to hand out."

He laughed softly. "You think that would have worked with my mother?"

"It's a better technique than mailing frightening photographs and then demanding information."

"I didn't send you that picture."

"I deal with liars every day of my life, Mr. Reyes. I know when I'm not getting the truth from someone."

"Then let me repeat myself." He came a step nearer. He was too close but Maya wouldn't allow herself to move as he spoke softly. "I did not send a photograph to you. Whatever you received, it did not come from my hands."

She felt a ripple of unease; he did seem to be telling her the truth.

"Then who sent it?" she asked.

"I don't know, but I intend to find out. If someone else knows your past, then they could be attempting to find your son, too. I want to know who it is."

His look was filled with such determination, she was instantly suspicious. "Why?"

"Why? Why not? If I were you, I'd be grateful for the help. Don't you want to know who sent you that picture?"

"I believe I already do."

"It wasn't me, Maya."

Her name, coming from his lips, sent another jolt down her body. To distract herself, she spoke again. "What about the other members of your family? Do they know what happened—"

"They know nothing of this situation and I intend to keep it that way. My father is very frail—if he were to think he had another grandson out there somewhere, his heart might not be able to take the stress of the search. The rest of the family would be equally upset. They'll accept the story I gave my mother." Better than any other explanation could have, the tone of his voice made Maya understand his position in the family. "They have no other choice."

Before she could reply, he spoke again. "What about you? How did you explain your absence to those at your firm?"

"I cited the case I gave Patricia."

"And your judgeship? How will your absence affect that situation?"

She didn't want to answer, but she did, his eyes pulling the words from her without her permission. "There is no comparison between a judgeship and your own flesh and blood. If my son is alive, I want to know."

"And then what?"

She'd thought long and hard about that question herself. The answer she'd come up with so far was the knowledge of what she *didn't* want to happen.

She didn't want him to become a Reyes.

"I'll deal with that when I need to," she said. "First I have to find out if he even exists. My motive in being here is to uncover the truth."

"Forgive me for pointing this out, but I believe the real reason you're here is that you want to keep your past a secret. Your way of handling the situation before now was to ignore it. The way you deal with matters is to run from them."

Her lips tightened as she started to argue with him. Then she thought better of it. Let him think what he wanted...why did she care? "Thank you for the analysis," she said. "I didn't know you were a psychologist."

"For all you know, I could be."

She blinked, then spoke calmly. "You hold a bachelor's degree in business administration from the University of Miami. You're forty-five and you've worked in your family's emerald mines since you were a teenager. You're in charge of the entire mining operation, but your oldest brother, Javier, is president of the company. You've been married once—it lasted two years—and now you're divorced. You have no children and you live here in your own wing of the villa." She paused, her eyes now challenging him. "Did I leave anything out?"

Still standing close, he acknowledged her research with a nod. "Very nice," he said smoothly. "You know a lot more than I suspected. Why don't you tell when I last made love to a beautiful woman?"

"I don't really care," she lied archly. "Your love life is the last thing I'm interested in exploring."

MARISOL RETURNED shortly after that and showed Maya to her room. "We have dinner at nine," she said. "My daughter and her family will eat with us as well as a few others. Feel free to come down when you've rested."

Dropping her purse on the nearest chair, Maya let her shoulders slump as Marisol closed the door behind her. Staying in the Reyes villa was the last thing Maya wanted to do. Why hadn't she simply refused? What could Shepard have done? He didn't want her identity exposed any more than she did at this point.

Fuming, Maya walked into the adjoining bedroom and looked around, then she acknowledged the real reason she'd given in. She'd done so…because she wanted to. She needed to see how the Reyes family lived and compare it to what Renaldo had told her all those years ago.

The truth she would never admit to was more complex and involved Shepard. Dammit to hell, she wanted to know more about him, too, even though she knew she shouldn't.

She crossed in front of a four-poster bed with a carved headboard and stepped to a window covered by dark drapes. The furniture and house were of the same vintage, an indeterminable time when heavy and ornate were in style. Pulling one velvet panel to the side, she looked down and into a courtyard that formed the center of the house. Lush with plants and blooms, Maya felt her heart lift despite the mess she was in.

This was what she missed—the rich, green beauty of Colombia. Raising her eyes to the mountains in the distance, her vision blurred. It'd been too many years since she'd seen the Andes and the sight of their towering peaks, even from this distance, touched her in a way she hadn't expected. She'd been so distressed over the trip itself she hadn't had time to think of how she might feel to see her country again. She wasn't prepared.

Turning away from the window, Maya sat down on the bed and closed her eyes, exhausted and confused but too wired to sleep.

It was dark when she woke up.

For a moment, she was totally disoriented, then she heard a bird cry outside and remembered where she was. Glancing at her watch, she was surprised to see she had slept away the afternoon and part of the evening, too. By the time she'd jumped from the bed, showered and did her hair and makeup, it was almost nine.

Downstairs, she found the dining room, but no one else had arrived. Spying a row of French doors that opened to the courtyard she'd seen from her window, she went to the nearest one and stepped outside to wait. Low lights lit the patio but the rest of the area stayed in darkness, the rich scent of a plumeria bush filling the night air. Maya walked across the cobbled brick toward a glass-topped table that sat on the edge of the patio, almost in darkness. Just as she reached for one of the chairs beside it, a slow, slithery motion beneath the table caught her eye.

An involuntary cry escaped her lips and she stumbled backward, stopping herself from falling at the very last minute.

Just then, a woman stepped from the shadows of the garden. Older than Maya, she wore heavy makeup and tight slacks, her high heels sinking into the grass as she followed Maya's gaze.

"You need to be careful." She waved a hand toward the table as her eyes returned to Maya's startled face. "There are many poisonous snakes here. The gardener tries to keep them away but some always slip through."

Maya swallowed, her heart still hammering. She looked back under the table but the snake was long gone.

The woman extended her hand. "I'm Luisa," she said. "Shepard's sister."

Maya took her fingers, noting the emerald ring she wore. The stone covered her knuckle. "How do you do. I'm Maya Velaquez."

"I know who you are. Shepard told us you were here."

Maya nodded, still a bit unsettled. Even though it made no sense, she couldn't help but wonder if there was a connection between Luisa's appearance and the snake's. Trying to sound friendly and put that thought behind her, Maya launched into her standard cocktail chitchat. Luisa replied to Maya's questions with one-word answers until Maya said, "So tell me, Luisa, what's your role in the family business?"

"I don't have one. I'm the daughter, and as such, I don't have an official capacity. Women in Colombia don't have brains, you know—"

Her bitter-sounding reply was cut short as a sudden thrashing pulled both women's attention to the foliage at the rear of the courtyard. A young boy appeared, his shirttail untucked, a smear of mud on the cuff of his trousers.

Luisa directed a stream of Spanish at him. Even if she hadn't spoken the language, Maya would have gotten the gist of her words. He was in big trouble. *Papá didn't like anyone looking messy at the dinner table, especially in front of guests.* Before the tirade could intensify, a man came out from the same direction Luisa herself had.

"Leave the boy alone," he said. "I told him I would race him here and he took the shortcut."

Luisa had seemed to appear from nowhere, but now, as Maya looked past the man, she could see the walkway she'd missed before. The darkness had concealed it.

"This is my husband, Esteban." Luisa gestured toward the man and then the boy. "And my son, Vincente."

Maya nodded toward them both.

The boy looked at her. "You're the lady Papá says will steal us all blind."

Luisa and her husband rushed to scold the boy.

"It's all right." Maya held up her hand to stop their fussing, but they continued until one of the French doors squeaked open and Shepard stepped out.

"Dinner is ready," he said. "Please come inside."

Maya quickly decided she wanted to do anything *but* follow him inside. Dressed in black, his shoulders filling the doorway, he suddenly seemed even more powerful and foreboding than he had back in the States. Her pulse, just beginning to slow from the snake sighting, took a leap back into overdrive.

Luisa and her family instantly obeyed, but Maya's feet seemed stuck to the patio.

Shepard let the door close behind the others, then he came to where she waited. She caught the faint scent of his aftershave in a breeze that swirled around them then fled.

He stared down at her and said nothing.

"I saw a snake," she said stupidly. "Over there, under the table."

He frowned and looked past her into the darkness. "What did it look like?"

"I—I don't know," she said. "It was a snake. Long, scary, yucky. Your sister said there are poisonous ones in the garden."

"There are," he confirmed. "You need to be careful." He paused. "Are you all right?"

"Of course," she said. "I screamed and it disappeared."

"I wasn't referring to *la serpiente*." He seemed to hesitate but she wondered if she imagined it. "I meant with what's about to happen. You meeting everyone. I didn't think about how stressful that would be until after I left you this afternoon. I'm sorry if I seemed…''

''Forget about it.'' She interrupted him, feeling uncomfortable with his apology. ''I can handle your family.''

His gaze held hers for longer than was necessary, then he took her elbow, leading her back inside.

CHAPTER SIX

SHEPARD HAD WANTED to study Javier as they entered, but his brother had yet to arrive and Shepard found himself grateful, whatever the delay. He wouldn't have been able to gauge Javier's reaction anyway—he was too busy staring at Maya himself.

She'd changed into a sleeveless black dress and had freed her hair. Hanging in soft waves just past her shoulders, the glimmer in the curls competed with the silver chain at her throat and the small diamonds in her ears. The simple attire was the perfect foil to her striking good looks, and as Shepard guided her toward the head of the table where his father sat, he wondered what was going on inside her head. Was she scared? Was she anxious? Was she angry?

Whatever combination of emotions she was experiencing, she kept them to herself, her face a mask of pleasant blandness.

Shepard made the introductions and Eduard studied Maya, his black marble eyes going over her, noting every detail. "So you're *la abogada* who's going to steal our money, eh?"

Shaking Eduard's hand, she smiled at his little joke. "That's certainly my intention," she said in a light voice. "But I'll leave a little…just for you."

He shook his head and pretended indignation. "You lawyers are all alike. Money, money, money. That is the reason for your very existence, no?"

"Perhaps," she replied. "But we come in handy when someone is needed to tend to the details."

To Shepard's amazement, a slow smile crossed his father's wizened face. "That's true," he conceded, "and when that someone is as beautiful as you, *señorita,* then the process is certainly less painful…" Without releasing Maya's hand, he waved toward Shepard's mother. "And you've met my wife already."

Maya nodded at Marisol. "Once again, I appreciate your hospitality, *señora.* Your home is lovely and you're very generous to share it with me."

Marisol acknowledged Maya's compliment. *"No hay de que,"* she murmured, turning back to Eduard's wheelchair. Shepard watched his mother fuss with the blanket Eduard had spread over his legs, their breakfast talk returning to his mind. He hadn't thought about the strange conversation and Shepard knew exactly why. He didn't *want* to think about it.

Shepard directed Maya to the other side of the

table where Minor Fuentes, the Reyes attorney waited, along with Teresa Montoya. Shepard gritted his teeth and made a sound under his breath. He had no idea his mother had included Teresa in their dinner plans.

Maya looked up at him in confusion. "Is something wrong?"

He didn't bother to hide his feelings. "Teresa is not my favorite person. I didn't know she was staying for dinner."

"You don't like her?"

"I don't trust her." Almost as an afterthought, he added, "She's a *santera*."

Maya's dark eyes widened then she shook her head. "The white dress...of course! I should have realized but it's been so long I guess I'd forgotten." She glanced at Shepard again. "Does her religion bother you?"

"I don't care if she bows down to potted plants, but my mother and sister believe she has special powers. And I can't seem to convince them otherwise."

His explanation broke off as they reached Teresa and Minor Fuentes. Maya shook the attorney's hand and nodded to Teresa then the dining room doors swung open to admit Javier.

Shepard watched his older brother cross the room, but if Javier had been the one who'd sent Maya the photo, he hid his guilt completely. Shepard introduced the two and his brother was nothing but charming.

They took their seats around the table and the maids brought in the first course.

"YOUR SPANISH IS EXCELLENT, *Señorita* Velaquez."

She'd made it through dinner and even dessert. Now the family had moved into the living room where coffee was being poured for everyone, including Vincente. The ritual was clearly ingrained and no one tried to bow out, even though it was well past midnight. Maya was grateful she'd had her nap.

She turned to the attorney, Minor Fuentes, who sat beside her on the sofa. He was a short, compact man, his dark hair shot through with silver, his gaze more intense, she saw now, than it appeared at first. He'd said little through dinner, his manner deferential to the family and polite to her.

"Where did you learn to speak the language?" His question seemed casual enough, but behind the inquiry, she caught a hint of nervousness. Did he think she was there to take his job?

"She learned it here." Gliding silently into the corner where they sat, Teresa Montoya answered for Maya. "You're from Colombia, no?"

Maya hid her surprise and nodded as the santera sat down in a nearby chair, her filmy white dress as elegant and ethereal as the woman herself. Maya found herself glancing across the room. She might be imagining things, but it seemed to her that the tension between Shepard and the santera went deeper than his simple explanation. Teresa was beautiful enough to catch any man's eye. Did she and Shepard have a history?

Maya gave herself a mental shake and answered the woman with the story she'd had ready, mixing the truth with lies. "I did grow up here. In a small village in the Andes. The farmers were unlucky, though. I doubt anyone lives there now."

"But their spirits may linger." Teresa focused her gaze on Maya's face and Maya felt as though the woman's green eyes were looking straight into her heart to read her lie. "If you inhabit a certain place for any length of time, your essence never completely leaves. Something of yourself is always there."

The man beside Maya chuckled anxiously. "I certainly hope that's not true, Teresa. I've traveled a lot—I fear I might have nothing of myself left, if that's the case."

"You fear everything, Sr. Fuentes." Shepard's older brother, Javier stepped into their circle, uninvited. He was smoking a cigar and as he spoke he jabbed it into the air, pointing to Teresa. "Tell him you lie, Teresa. It isn't good to scare old men."

"You're right, Javier." Fuentes laughed too loudly and too quickly. His reaction told Maya how conscious he was of Javier and his place in the family. "Absolutely right."

"No, he isn't." Although Teresa's voice was as soft as it'd been before, Maya caught something else in it as she spoke. An edge as sharp as the one on Maya's pocketknife at home. She flicked her thumb over the bandage on her palm, the thought coming to her all at once that she'd been wrong to imagine Teresa and Shepard together. The tension between the santera and Javier was almost visible.

Teresa interrupted Maya's thoughts, her words confirming her suspicions even more. "Javier is completely wrong and he knows it."

Javier's eyes narrowed but he didn't speak. Smiling with the satisfaction of a sleek, white cat, Teresa rose. "His own soul abandoned him many years ago. It's high in the mountains and he'll never get it back. Someday we'll all know why..."

With those astonishing words, she left the group. A second later, Minor Fuentes looked into his coffee cup as if just now noticing it was empty and murmuring his apologies, he stood and fled.

Maya pondered the santera's strange pronouncement, then dismissed it. She had other things more important to consider than where Javier Reyes's soul might be. She compared him, just as she had Shepard, to her memories of Renaldo.

Save for the color of his dark hair and eyes, Javier bore no resemblance to either of his siblings. As tall as Shepard but heavier, he did seem to share the same arrogance his younger brother had had, but without Renaldo's grace. Uneasy because of his silent nearness and sullen expression, Maya sat quietly and waited. Javier continued to smoke, then finally he turned to her. His initial gaze felt cold, but it changed so quickly, Maya wasn't sure.

"What do you intend to accomplish here, *señorita?*"

"I intend to accomplish whatever your brother wants," she said in a calm voice. "He's the one who invited me to see the mine. I'll be at his disposal."

He stared at her through a smoky blue haze. "I am the one who runs Muzo."

"I understand that." Boxed in, there was little else she could say. "I'd be more than happy to discuss our proposal with you when and if we are able to work out the details."

"And how long will it take you to…work out the details?"

"I suppose, again, that depends on your brother."

"On Shepard?"

"Unless you mean someone else…" Too late, she realized the implication of her words.

"We did have another brother." He drew deeply on the cigar. "His name was Renaldo. He died eighteen years ago."

It was easy to look shocked—she hadn't expected Renaldo's name to be brought up and she wasn't prepared. "I'm very sorry to hear that."

"I'm sorry you heard it, too."

Appearing unexpectedly, Shepard stood before them, a fierce frown marring his expression as he repeated her words. "It isn't necessary to burden *Señorita* Velaquez with our family history, Javier." His dark eyes turned to hers. "Please accept my apologies on his behalf."

Javier didn't move…or speak. A million replies went through Maya's brain but all of them sounded awkward. Shepard saved her from answering.

He held out his hand. "My father is retiring. He wants to wish you a good evening."

"Of course." Relief flooded Maya as she took Shepard's fingers. Javier was not an easy person to be around but she had the feeling he liked it that way. He wanted to intimidate.

Shepard directed her to the hallway where his father waited, his mother at the ready behind the wheelchair.

"Thank you for gracing our table this evening,

señorita.'' Eduard smiled and motioned for her to come closer. She leaned down and he brushed both her cheeks with lips that felt like paper. ''I want to talk to you in the morning about the foolishness of my son. You'll have breakfast with me and the two of us will discuss it further.''

His words were not an invitation. They were a command.

''I'd be happy to.'' She should have thought a little more about the excuse Shepard had come up with for her presence. She hadn't been prepared for everyone to be so interested. She should have known better.

''Bueno,'' he said. ''I eat at ten. On the patio.'' He then motioned to his wife and she began to push his chair down the hallway. Shepard and Maya watched until they disappeared around the corner.

''Come outside with me,'' Shepard said. His voice held as much room for argument as his father's had.

''Not now. I've had enough for one evening—''

As if she hadn't spoken, he took her arm in his and pulled her through the nearest set of doors to the patio. Suddenly they were in the dark, the smell of gardenias strong, his fingers biting into her arm.

Shepard cut her protest off before it could start. ''What did my brother say to you? Did he ask you about the store? How did you answer?''

His barrage of questions took her by surprise, but not as much as the ripple of awareness she felt at his closeness. Responding to him in a way she would have never anticipated, Maya frowned. Then, with shock, she understood.

How many times had she stood in the dark with Renaldo, his hands on her skin, their words spoken in whispers, their proximity measured in heartbeats? A hundred? A thousand? Too many to count.

She swayed, the memory so strong it seemed more real than the present.

Shepard tightened his grip and she pulled back from him, or rather tried to, but he continued to hold on to her.

"Let me go," she demanded. "I don't want—"

All at once, the door behind them creaked open. Maya twisted to see Javier step out of the house, the tip of his cigar glowing. His eyes caught her movement and in a flash, he took in the situation.

Anyone else would have apologized. Javier simply stared.

Shepard broke the silence. "Did you need something?"

"No." He held up his cigar. "I came out to enjoy the last of my wicked pleasure." His eyes washed over Maya. "I'm sorry to have interrupted your own."

Maya spoke quickly. "This isn't what—"

Shepard squeezed her wrist so tightly she almost cried out. Then she fell silent. Which was exactly what he wanted.

"You haven't interrupted anything." Shepard's voice was as smooth as the arm he slipped around Maya's waist. Hugging her to him, he spoke in Spanish to his brother, the words flying too fast for even Maya to catch. Javier laughed once, a short, ugly sound, then he shot her a measuring glance and went inside, leaving the two of them alone again.

Maya pivoted, her gaze colliding with Shepard's. She didn't know which disturbed her more—his closeness, her reaction, or what had just transpired between him and his brother. "What do you think you're doing?"

He no longer held her arm, but Shepard's eyes held her just as tightly. "My brother is not a man to be trifled with, Maya. If he thinks we're lovers, all the better. He probably respects that kind of relationship more than any other."

"I don't understand—"

"And you don't need to." In a heartbeat, he was closer, although she hadn't seen him move. His breath brushed her cheek as he spoke. "Be wary of him, Maya. Be very wary. He's not the person he appears to be." He paused to let her absorb his warning, then said, "Now, tell me what he asked you…"

Thirty minutes later, Maya crawled in bed after giving Shepard an account of his brother's questions. He'd listened closely, nodding once or twice, his face a blank other than that. She fell asleep with Shepard's words ringing in her ears. *He's not the person he appears to be.*

Who is, she wondered, half awake, half asleep. *Who is?*

SHEPARD NEEDED very little rest; in fact, he did his best thinking between one and three in the morning. Standing outside his wing of the villa an hour after everyone else had gone to bed, he stared at the window of Maya's bedroom, the breeze whispering around him. Maya had no idea what she was getting into and if he had a heart inside his body, he'd put her on the next flight back to the States.

But he didn't have a heart. And Maya Vega was a grown woman. She'd made the decision to come here on her own, so why shouldn't he take advantage of her presence? He'd use her to find Renaldo's son, if he was even alive, and once that was done, he'd send her home. All Shepard wanted from her was her help.

Or was it?

He could still feel the impression her curves had left against him while they'd been in the garden. He'd been surprised by her softness; the hard edges of her personality had deceived him into expecting the same from her body.

Since his divorce, Shepard had had little time for women. He'd dated, of course, and had turned down nothing that had been offered to him, but he'd had no serious relationships. At least not the kind a woman like Maya Vega would expect.

He shook his head, then drained the last of the drink he'd come outside to finish. What the hell was he doing, thinking of her in those terms? She wasn't what he'd thought but she *had* been his brother's lover and he needed to remember that. Any woman who could be with a man like Renaldo was a woman Shepard would never understand. Even if he wanted to.

With Maya still on his mind, he started to go back into the house then suddenly he stopped.

Somewhere inside the villa a woman was screaming.

MAYA THOUGHT she was having the dream again. Her heart thumping against her rib cage, she woke to a frightening sound, but what? She listened closely, expecting to hear, as usual, the sound of a crying child but when the noise repeated itself, she realized she wasn't dreaming. She'd heard a woman's screams.

Jumping from her bed, she grabbed her robe and

ran to the door, throwing it open to look up and down the empty hallway. She had no idea where the other bedrooms were, but it suddenly didn't matter. Another cry came from her right, and Maya ran toward it, a flickering light beckoning her from the corner of the corridor.

Running around the turn, her bare feet slapping the cold terrazzo floor, she saw Marisol at the end of the hallway, Luisa and Esteban beside her. Shepard's brother-in-law was holding his wife but she was resisting him, her loud distraught voice making it clear who had screamed. As Maya reached the group, Shepard came into the hallway from an adjacent room.

"What's wrong?" she asked breathlessly. "I heard someone scream—"

Luisa broke away from her husband and stormed toward Maya. For one passing second Maya thought Shepard's sister was actually going to slap her. Maya flinched, and Luisa seemed to have second thoughts. She stopped short and yelled at her instead.

"This is all your fault! You shouldn't have come here. You upset him and now look at what's happened!"

Her tirade continued as Shepard strode to Maya's side. They exchanged a quick glance—hers, one of utter confusion, his own, one of anger—before he turned swiftly to his sister and drilled her with the sternest of looks.

She fell silent, but just for a moment. "You don't belong here!" Pointing a shaking finger at Maya, Luisa glared. "If my father dies, it's all your fault!"

"Luisa! *¡Silencio!*" Shepard spoke harshly and Luisa finally stopped. He turned to Maya. "My father has had a heart attack," he explained. "His nurses are with him. The ambulance is on its way."

"Oh, my God, Shepard!" Maya put a hand to her lips, her mouth falling open in shock. "I'm so sorry. Will he—will he be all right?"

"We'd better pray so," he answered cryptically. He started to say more but the maid called out from downstairs, her voice echoing up the stairwell.

"They're here! The ambulance has arrived!"

In short order, three men in dark blue uniforms bounded up the stairway, a stretcher carried between them as they hurried into the bedroom. Maya caught a glimpse of Eduard as they rushed out a few minutes later. He lay still and motionless, his face matching the white blanket someone had draped over him.

Marisol and the others followed the paramedics, Luisa sending a last withering look at Maya before she joined the procession. Shepard came to where she waited, his hand poised on the polished brass handrail.

"Are you okay?" he asked.

Considering the situation, his concern touched her in a way it shouldn't have.

"I'm fine," she answered quickly. "But I'm getting a hotel room in the morning. Your sister's so upset with me, I can't stay here any longer."

"Absolutely not. Don't even consider leaving," he said. "She needs to blame someone and you happened to be handy." He spoke again, his voice lower. "There's nothing any of us can do. Go back to bed and try to get some rest. I'll call you from the hospital. And one last thing…"

"Yes?" She looked down at him.

"While we're gone, keep your door locked. The guard's out front but we've had some break-ins." His expression tightened imperceptibly. "It's just a precaution. ¿*Entiende?*"

She nodded then watched him jog down the marble stairway. *Keep the door locked? We've had break-ins?* At the bottom, he stopped one more time and turned around to stare at her.

She wanted to run and hide, but she couldn't. Shepard's eyes wouldn't let her. He held her gaze for a long second, then finally—regretfully, it appeared—he broke eye contact and hurried away, the front door slamming behind him.

In the ringing silence, Maya realized her knees were not working right. Feeling weak, she leaned against the stair railing and named the emotion she was experiencing. Fear.

But she didn't know which frightened her the most—the warning she'd just received or the man who had delivered it.

CHAPTER SEVEN

MAYA FOUND HER WAY BACK to her room and went inside, locking the door behind her just as Shepard had instructed. Crawling between the heavy cotton sheets, she glanced at the clock. It was 3:00 a.m. Shepard had still been in the clothes he'd worn to dinner. Had he not gone to bed at all? What had he been doing?

With his warning ringing in her mind, Maya was sure she wouldn't go back to sleep. Exhaustion took over, however, and within minutes she was out. A few hours later, just as the sun rose and slipped in through her windows, she woke again, her heart jumping into her throat. This time she *knew* she'd been dreaming. The room was empty but she'd imagined a man standing by her bed. Just standing and watching her sleep.

She stumbled into the shower and after she'd washed her hair and stood under the hot spray for a full ten minutes she realized Shepard had never called. Turning off the water, she reached for a towel and hoped he'd gotten too busy to phone and nothing more serious had happened.

Maya chastised herself as she began to dress. She should be taking advantage of Shepard's absence, not wondering what he was doing. After donning a long skirt and a turtleneck, she retrieved a leather notebook from her briefcase then sat down at the desk situated under the window. The phone at her side, she dialed the first number on the action list she'd drawn up while still in Houston.

Two hours later, she had everything arranged. Tomorrow morning by this time, she'd be on her way to Punto Perdido. If Renita had been the woman who'd come to Shepard, Maya had a lot of questions for her aunt. The trip would help her seek those answers *and* it'd take her away from Shepard for the day, a very good thing. The morning light was bright as it poured through the window where she sat, but she shivered suddenly, remembering his eyes—and his warning—from the night before. Had they really had break-ins or did he fear that Luisa might harm Maya? The notion seemed absurd, especially now, but who could say? This was, after all, Colombia. Anything was possible.

Maya had only a moment to ponder that point before someone knocked. She crossed the room and paused by the door. Shepard spoke from the other side.

"It's me. Open up."

Maya threw the ancient brass bolt and twisted the knob.

His appearance shook her. Clearly exhausted, he was leaning against the door frame, his shoulders slumped, his tie undone. There were circles of fatigue beneath his eyes and rough stubble dotted his jaw and cheeks.

His hair looked as if he'd run his hand through it a thousand times.

Sympathy rose inside her. "Oh, Shepard… You look so weary. Is your father all right?"

"He's going to survive. He informed me before I left the hospital that he's too mean to die."

Maya felt relief. For years, she'd hated the Reyes family, but last night, when she'd met the old man, she'd felt a connection with him she couldn't shake, no matter how hard she tried. He had a stubbornness about him that had appealed to her.

Shepard moved past her to the sofa where he sat down and stretched his long legs before him, closing his eyes with a sigh.

"I'm glad he'll be all right," Maya said. "I was worried. It was a heart attack?"

"The doctors believe it might have been a mild one." Shepard opened his eyes. "They need tests to confirm the diagnosis but when they told him what they entailed, he began to argue over whether they were necessary.''

"What! He has to find out—"

Shepard waved a hand, dismissing her words. "You obviously don't know my father, Maya. He needs no information to make a decision. He believes he already has all the facts.''

"But he's not a doctor," she said in dismay.

"It doesn't matter. The truth is irrelevant. Reality is what he makes it." He paused. "Sound familiar?"

She knew he referred to Renaldo, but she refused to take the bait.

"I'm just glad he's going to be all right," she said quietly. "That's the most important thing."

"Of course. You're right…" He scrubbed his face with his hands, then shook his head as if to clear it. "I've arranged for nurses, but my mother insisted on staying with him. I'll have to send a car for her later or she'll never leave."

Maya nodded, then she had to ask the question that had been troubling her since the early morning disaster. "Shepard, about Luisa… Tell me the truth. Were you worried about burglars or her last night?"

He sidestepped her question. "Luisa isn't as…stable as she first appears. I didn't want to take a chance."

"I can take care of myself."

"I didn't mean to imply you couldn't. But there are circumstances here of which you know nothing. It would be to your advantage to let me guide you."

Something in his speech set off her radar and Maya thought of the trip she had planned for tomorrow. Her eyes jerked to the desk where her papers were still spread. He couldn't know of the arrangements she'd made, could he? Not this quickly...

Suddenly she'd had enough dancing around the topic.

"Why don't you say what you really mean? You don't want to 'guide' me. You want to keep tabs on me and make sure you know if I find my son."

"I *do* want to find him," he answered, his reply as candid as her question. "But Colombia is a dangerous place, a place where you could need help and not get it. This house is no exception. You're safer here than at a hotel but if someone wanted to harm you while we were all gone, the maids would never hear."

Rising from the couch, he walked to the window beside the desk and stared down into the jungle-like garden. "I'm not the only person who knows who you are, Maya." He turned to face her. "Whoever sent that photograph sent it for a reason. It was a warning, plain and simple. We have to remember that. We have to be careful."

She stood, too, and crossed her arms. "There's no 'we' to this situation. If my son lives, you'll have nothing to do with him, Shepard."

"He's a Reyes."

"No. He's not a Reyes. I wasn't married to your brother."

"I'm not talking about a piece of paper. I'm talking about blood."

"And I'm talking about a person. A real, honest-to-God living person, not another example of the Reyeses' heritage. If I find him, he'll have nothing to do with your family."

He stood so still he could have been made of stone. "You surprise me. If I didn't know better, I would think those words had come from my brother's lips, not yours."

"I'm not a stranger to your history. I know the real story behind your wealth and power."

"And you got those facts from my brother—"

"No. I got them for myself. I wanted the truth, not the rhetoric Renaldo believed."

"And what are these so-called facts?"

"The Reyeses operate a mining concern that is dangerous and risky. It provides the primary source of employment for many of the surrounding villages, so you have no trouble getting workers. But they have no benefits or even decent wages, and you take advantage of their inability to find other jobs. In addition, you've managed to placate…or bribe…every mining minister who's been in power, except for the current one. You manipulate the government and its people to benefit your bank account and you always will.''

His face darkened and he moved closer to her, so close she could see the fine lines that fanned from the corners of his eyes. A woman would have tried to cover them up with makeup but they added to Shepard's good looks. Remembering the last time he'd stood this near—in the garden the night before—she willed her body not to react.

It didn't listen.

Her mouth went dry, and her pulse accelerated. When Shepard reached out and lifted her chin with his thumb, her heart sped up even more.

''You paint with a very wide brush, Maya Vega.''

She couldn't answer him. Her breath had deserted her, disappearing into a vortex of confusion and attraction. This couldn't be happening, she told herself. Why was she acting like this?

His head dipped lower and their eyes were almost even. A tremor rippled down her spine before she could stop it.

''Some of us are honorable,'' he said tightly.

"And some of us are not. You might do well to figure out who's who before you condemn us all."

SHEPARD LEFT Maya's room with his irritation barely in check. She clearly thought little of his family but he didn't care. That wasn't what had angered him.

No, he was upset with himself, not her. Standing there in the morning light, her unmade bed four steps away, he'd been unable to think of anything but picking her up and carrying her to those rumpled covers. He imagined the scent of her skin and the warmth of her body lingering in the tangled sheets.

Hurrying down the hallway, Shepard curbed his thoughts with a will made of steel. He had no business thinking of Maya like this. His response was as inappropriate as it was pointless. If he needed to remind himself of that, all he had to do was remember she'd loved his brother.

And the proof of what that meant had been scattered across her desk. He'd glanced at the papers when she hadn't been looking. She'd made all the necessary arrangements to travel into the mountains in the morning, her driver hired, her route mapped out. She obviously had no plans to ask him to accompany her or she would have said something.

Shepard entered his father's room and hurriedly gathered the personal things he'd requested, thinking all the while how Eduard's medical crisis had changed things. The situation was now more urgent than ever and Shepard's determination took another leap. Finding Renaldo's son had to take precedence over everything.

Heading out the door, Shepard ran into his sister.

She gasped and dropped the file she'd been carrying, papers flying to the polished floor. "Shepard! You scared me half to death!"

"I'm sorry, Luisa. I was rushing around, not watching what I was doing…" He bent to collect the loose sheets, seeing, in the process, that they were the latest output reports from the Muzo. One knee still on the floor, he held the papers and looked up at her in surprise. "What is this? Why do you have these?"

She snatched the documents from his fingers and clearly tried to think of an excuse. When one didn't come, her shoulders slumped. "I was helping Esteban," she confessed. "He…hasn't had time to work on these so I told him I would do them for him."

Shepard stood up slowly. "Those are complicated reports, Luisa—"

"I know that." She flushed, her defensiveness rising to the surface. "But I've done them before."

Shepard couldn't contain his amazement. Luisa's interest in the business had always been limited to what she could steal from the take, or so he'd thought.

"You don't have to look so surprised," she said

quietly. "I've been teaching Vincente the business. I do have a brain, you know."

"It wasn't that—"

"Some day, my son will work in the company, Shepard, so I need to prepare him for what's coming. You won't allow Esteban to do anything important like run the new store, but that won't be the case with Vincente."

Marisol's warning rang in Shepard's mind. She'd been right, he thought in amazement. Luisa was opposing the store just because she thought Shepard was going to run it himself. The excuse he'd picked for this charade was becoming troublesome.

"Luisa, please… It isn't a case of allowing anything. Esteban can't handle the work he's got, much less open a retail outlet in another country."

"That's your opinion," she said, tossing her long, dark hair. "You're wrong, but even if that doesn't matter to you, I'd think you'd care about Papá." She tilted her head toward Maya's end of the hallway. "If she hadn't been here last night, he wouldn't have had that attack."

"That's ridiculous, Luisa. Maya had nothing to do with what happened."

"How do you know? She obviously upset him." She bit her bottom lip, her thick lipstick staining her teeth. "This whole business about…about the store," she stuttered. "He doesn't want to do that."

"He might, you never know. He liked Maya."

Her eyes widened. "That's impossible."

"Why is that impossible, Luisa?" he asked slowly. "Maya's articulate, intelligent…not unattractive… Papá isn't dead yet, you know. He can appreciate those things in someone, especially a woman."

"It's just…just not possible," Luisa sputtered. She gathered her papers closer, gave him a final look then went on down the hall.

The day passed in a blur of work and confusion. Late that night, after he'd insisted his mother come home from the hospital, Shepard took his drink in hand and stepped outside, his eyes on Maya's window, his thoughts on the curious conversation he'd had with his sister. Her reaction to Maya made no sense. If Luisa was smart enough to compile those reports for Esteban, then she was smart enough to know he couldn't handle the responsibility of a store. Was love that blind?

Finishing his drink, Shepard went back inside, the answer to his rhetorical question coming to him abruptly as he lay in bed. Why he'd never considered the possibility until this very moment, he had no idea; it seemed obvious now.

If Maya and Renaldo's son was never found and Shepard and Javier died without heirs, Vincente, Luisa's child, would inherit everything.

Suddenly wide awake, Shepard stared in the darkness at the ceiling.

Maybe there were others besides his brother he needed to worry about....

MAYA SIPPED her morning tea and tried not to look anxious. Shepard and his mother had just left the breakfast table and were supposed to be on their way to the hospital shortly. Glancing down at her watch, she hoped they hurried. She was scheduled to meet her car and driver five blocks from the house in less than ten minutes. If she wasn't there on time, she wasn't sure the man would wait.

Rising from the table as if she had nothing else to do, she went to her room where she picked up her coat and purse and prepared to leave. When she came down the stairs a few minutes later, she glanced out an upper window and saw Shepard's dark vehicle pull away from the courtyard. Hurrying to the front door, she stepped into the chilly morning. The sky was loaded with dark clouds and in the higher elevations where she was headed, the temperatures would be even cooler, the rain heavier. She pulled her scarf from her bag and covered her hair as she walked quickly toward the security gate, refusing to give in to her urge to look over her shoulder.

Head down, step determined, she quickly reached

the end of the block, the wind whistling past her, scattering leaves and trash before her path. She plowed through the mess, her attention focused on the corner where the driver had promised to wait. A large SUV edged to the curb just as she reached the intersection.

She glanced in both directions and started across the street.

That's when she realized her mistake.

CHAPTER EIGHT

MAYA DREW EVEN with the black Expedition, and Shepard leaned across the front seat to open the door. Her expression held anger and disappointment. A tinge of fear was there, as well. Her reaction was something he could use to his advantage, but the fact that she was frightened of him didn't feel as good as he would have expected.

"Are you going somewhere?" he asked.

There was no sense in lying and she knew it. Still, she hesitated.

"Get in," he ordered.

She climbed inside, the car's warm air and fogged windows creating a sense of intimacy that grew when her perfume drifted across the seat. It smelled like honeysuckle and under different circumstances, Shepard would have let himself enjoy it. But not now. Not here. Not with this woman.

"Why didn't you tell me your plans for today?" He kept his features and his voice as neutral as possible, but she moved imperceptibly toward the car door she'd just entered, her fingers returning to the handle.

"I assumed you would be at the hospital with your father. I didn't want to trouble you—"

"Don't." He held up his hand and she fell silent. "Lies will get you nowhere. I saw the papers on your desk yesterday morning." He put the vehicle in gear and made a U-turn.

Her voice gave no hint of her anxiousness, but it was there. Shepard could sense it, right behind the facade of her defiance. "Where are you taking me?" she said.

"Where you want to go," he answered. "Punto Perdido. I assume that's where your aunt now lives?"

Maya frowned, then answered. "She's always lived there. I grew up in Punto Perdido."

He sent her a sharp look. "Renaldo said you were from Mitu, near the Brazilian border."

She shook her head. "He lied…but no one told the truth back then. Our lives depended on it."

"No wonder none of my people could locate your aunt." Shepard spoke, then silently cursed his brother's paranoia, knowing at the same time those precautions had kept Renaldo living for as long as he had. "We searched the border relentlessly but had no luck. We never looked closer."

Maya stewed in silence for several miles, then

seemed to decide she'd take advantage of the chance to grill him, her background too ingrained for anything else. She softened him up with a few easy questions, then slipped a harder one in. "You know, you never explained what brought Renita to your office in the first place. Why don't you tell me more about that…"

He felt sudden pity for the hapless witnesses Maya cross-examined. "I did a favor for your aunt and she said she wanted to pay me back."

"What kind of favor?"

He hesitated but there was no reason not to tell her. "I've established clinics in some of the villages. A year ago, she took her child to one and the doctors found a heart problem. The boy was brought to Bogota where he could get the surgery."

She looked skeptical.

"She told me she wanted to thank me," he explained. "For the life of her son. I didn't seek her out, Maya. She came to see me at my office in Muzo."

"Well, she paid you back with lies. And I want to know why. Clearly I can do that better on my own than with you beside me."

He shook his head. "I disagree. I can help you. Why won't you let me?"

"Because I don't trust you, that's why."

"I want the same thing you do—to find your son if he lives."

"Yes, but *why?*" she asked, turning to him. "He would be your nephew and I understand that, but there's more to the story, isn't there?"

"Does there need to be more?"

"I don't know if there *needs* to be. But something tells me there *is.*"

"The situation is not that simple. And even if it was, you're better off not knowing."

"That's never the case." She shook her head, her expression set. "The more information you have, the better your decisions."

"Really?" He cut his eyes to hers. "If you'd known how it was going to turn out, would you still have loved my brother?"

"I'm not sure," she said after a silent moment. "Our situation didn't end well…but I think it was meant to be."

"Fated lovers? You don't believe in that kind of nonsense, do you?"

"I must. I can't imagine having any other kind of life and that was all set in motion by knowing Renaldo."

"You make it sound as if you did nothing to shape your own existence."

"I'm not sure I did," she said.

"What about your hard work? All your efforts?"

She shrugged. "What about yours? You're clearly the one who runs your family's business yet Javier is the man in charge, or so he told me."

Shepard tightened his jaw. "I'm happy doing what I do. I don't need recognition."

"And he does?"

Shepard gripped the leather-wrapped steering wheel and stared through the windshield. "What my brother needs is anyone's guess. I wouldn't dream of answering that question."

His reply ended the discussion. Maya stared out the window and the silence between them deepened but the lack of conversation didn't bother Shepard; he needed to concentrate on his driving. The closer they got to the village, the higher they went, and the worse the roads became. Without the SUV, they would never have made it. After an hour, Shepard spotted a small sign pointing toward a road heading north. He turned and thirty minutes later, the Expedition entered a typical square around which every village in Colombia seemed centered. A cathedral, of sorts, was on one side, a set of low government buildings occupied another, and retail establishments—tiny *bodegas* and even smaller cafés—lined the remaining edges. A few cars were parked along the street, but most of the vehicles were trucks or SUVs, all of an uncertain vintage. A cluster of shoe-shine boys huddled in the square, wool coats fashioned of blankets draped across their skinny shoulders.

Shepherd turned to Maya. Her face had paled so much, her brown eyes looked darker and larger than usual. He'd obviously found the right village.

AFTER STANDING before countless juries, Maya had learned to keep her emotions under control and her expressions guarded. That ability seemed to have fled the moment she returned to Colombia, however. She felt as if she were revealing every feeling, every reaction, every thought, that crossed her mind. Her doubt regarding Shepard's story about Renita had been obvious. He wasn't the kind of man who'd build hospitals for the poor. A Reyes wouldn't do something like that.

She stared at the square, knowing her face reflected the turmoil she was experiencing.

"It hasn't changed. Not a bit..." Her voice sounded strained, even to her own ears. "It's as if I never left...."

"Do you want to get out?"

"In a minute," she said. "Let me look first."

He said nothing and sat quietly, his patience, unlike most American men's, apparently unending.

Maya let the scene envelop her, the sights and sounds so similar to what they'd been eighteen years before, it was almost eerie. The church, the stores, even the building that housed *el departamento de la policía*…it all looked the same. The church bells began to peal the hour and Maya inhaled deeply. She'd been holding her breath, she realized, as an acrid smoke suddenly filled her senses. The smell of it turned her stomach.

She closed her eyes but it did no good. She still knew where she was.

"What can I do to make this easier for you?"

Shepard's question was so obvious Maya knew he asked it just to break the pain-filled silence. But whether or not his concern was sincere, she didn't care. She was suddenly grateful for his solid presence and the deep timbre of his voice. If she'd been alone, she might have turned around and fled, gaining nothing but pain.

"There's nothing anyone can do. It…it's very hard," she said thickly. "Harder than I'd expected."

"Your life here was not good."

She turned to him so she wouldn't have to look out the window. "I came to Punto Perdido because I had nowhere else to go. When I was twelve, my parents were ambushed and killed by bandits on the road between our village and here. Renita and Segundo were all the relatives I had. Segundo told me many times how lucky I was that they took me."

Something crossed Shepard's face that she

couldn't read. "You said back in Houston that he was not a good person. What did you mean?"

From the day she'd moved in with them, Maya had heard the fights and seen the bruises on Renita's body. Segundo had slapped Maya more than once, too, but when Renaldo had found out, he'd put a quick stop to it. His intervention had embarrassed her uncle but she'd been glad. Hitting hadn't been the only thing Segundo had wanted to do to her.

"He was cruel to my aunt," she said shortly.

She returned her gaze to the window, staring toward a dusty side street where three dogs fought over the contents of a spilled trash can. "When I left here, I vowed I'd never return. I don't like going back on my word, even when no one knows but me."

"You're too hard on yourself," Shepard chastised her gently.

"No. I'm a very weak woman and a liar, as well." Maya looked down at her hands. "I said I'd never return and here I am." Her throat burned. "And I said I didn't care, but I still do."

He reached across the leather seat and covered her hands with his fingers. They were broad and strong-looking, the nails neatly trimmed, his skin a rich, dark brown. She wanted to pull away from his touch but the reassuring weight of his grip was simply too welcome. She drew strength from it, strength and comfort, the other issues between them unimportant for the moment.

"You aren't a liar and you aren't weak. There are many words I would use to describe you, Maya, but those two would not be included."

She couldn't help herself; she looked into his eyes. The mistake was a big one. They were lit with a warmth that raised her temperature far too quickly. "What words would you use?" she asked without thinking.

"Inteligente. Hermosa." His voice, unbelievably, was teasing and light and she knew he was trying to lift her spirits. Then he came to his final word and he said it with reluctance. *"Y espantada."*

He'd seen the fear she'd tried to hide. Despite this obvious fact, she made an effort to bluff her way past him. "You're mistaken. Why would I be frightened?"

"Because you should be," he said quietly. "If you don't let me help you, this search will not go as you want. Instead of your son, you'll end up finding more trouble than you can even imagine."

HIS WORDS SEEMED to mean little to her. Maya nodded then opened the car door and stepped outside. He followed, meeting her on the sidewalk.

She tilted her head to her right. "We'll walk this

direction. That way we can pass the midwife's house.''

The wind was harsh and cold, buffeting them with gusts that threatened to knock them off stride. Shepard thought briefly of putting his arm around Maya's waist but he dismissed the idea and settled for a hand against the small of her back. Beneath his palm, she tensed but she didn't pull away.

Punto Perdido was as poor and barren as Shepard had expected. He frequently visited the homes of his miners and he knew the situation well. He was doing what he could to break the cycle but it was a constant battle. Eduard and Javier vetoed every type of assistance he proposed.

They walked in silence, Maya's feet slowing as they approached one of the smaller, stucco homes.

"This is where the midwife lived. Amarilla Rodriguez. I wonder if she's still there.''

The wind blew the sound of laughter to where Maya and Shepard paused. Seconds later, a gaggle of children—none wearing coats or even shoes—rushed around the corner of the house and tumbled into the front yard, capturing the puppy they'd been chasing. A woman followed. Somewhere between twenty and forty—her age was impossible to guess—but she wasn't the midwife, that much was clear. Maya approached her and asked for Amarilla.

"I don't know anyone by that name," the woman said quickly.

Maya started to press her, but one of the children began to scream and the woman ran to see what was wrong.

"That wasn't her?" Shepard asked.

"No. The midwife was a hundred years old when she delivered my child!" She made a wry face. "At least that's how old she seemed to me at the time. She was probably the age I am right now, or maybe a little older. She'd just had a baby herself."

They continued on their way, Maya's steps growing slower and slower the farther they got from the square. As they neared the end of the second block, she stopped altogether. Shepard followed her stare to a house across the way.

He amended himself immediately. The place hardly qualified as a house. The more proper word would have been shack. Unpainted concrete blocks formed the walls and tin, nailed haphazardly, served as the roof. The porch was three feet, maybe four, back from the sidewalk. The area between wasn't really a yard, but it *was* neatly swept, two pots of greenery on either side of the packed dirt leading to the door.

Maya stood motionless, then she exhaled softly a second later, her face reflecting a pain so deep and awful, Shepard couldn't help but wince. He spoke despite himself.

"Why don't you go back to the truck? Let me—"

"Let you accuse me of running away again?" She shook her head, her eyes glinting. "I don't think so. I've come this far. I can handle the rest of it."

THE INSIDE OF THE HOUSE was dark. When the door was opened at her knock, Maya couldn't see the person who'd pulled it back. She squinted, her question hesitant. "I'm looking for Renita Alvarez. Does she still live here?"

Her name was spoken so softly, Maya didn't catch it the first time. "Maya? *¿Eso es tú? ¿Realmente?*"

Despite the years and all the heartache that had passed since she'd heard it last, the voice was instantly familiar to Maya. She took two steps forward and held out both hands. "Renita!"

The women embraced on the porch, Maya shocked at how frail and thin…and old her aunt had become. Ten years separated them, but the time had been less kind to Renita. As Maya drew back, she could hardly believe her eyes.

If Renita noticed her niece's surprise, she gave no indication. Instead, her gaze darted over Maya's shoulder to Shepard. For a second, Maya thought her aunt might jump back inside the house and lock the door, then her eyes returned to Maya, their brown depths filling so fast they quickly overflowed. "I'm sorry, Maya… I'm so sorry…."

Maya wrapped her arms around Renita again. "It's all right," she murmured, "it's all right…"

Somehow they made it inside the tiny dwelling. A little boy of five, maybe six, came into the main room from the back. The resemblance to Renita was obvious but before Maya could even greet the child, her aunt sent him out the door with instructions to go to the neighbors.

Maya and Shepard took seats at a table Maya remembered, Renita's tears continuing as she fixed coffee and offered them fresh bread. Maya asked about the boy. Was he the one who'd benefited from Shepard's clinic?

Renita nodded, almost reluctantly. "His father was a good man, but he's dead," she said bluntly. "There was gunfire one morning. When he went to the window, he was hit."

By the way Renita spoke, Maya instantly understood Segundo hadn't been the child's father. He was obviously gone and had been for some time. What had happened to him? Had he left? Was he dead, too? Maya decided not to ask. For whatever reason, her uncle was no longer an issue and that was fine with her.

"Who shot him?" Shepard asked gently. "The soldiers or the rebels?"

Renita shrugged. She didn't know and she didn't care. He was gone, what else mattered?

Reaching across the table to touch her aunt's

hand, Maya spoke softly. "Renita, I know this is hard for you. It's hard for me, as well. But I need to find out more about what you told *Señor* Reyes." Her mouth was so dry she had to stop and take a sip of the coffee before she could continue. A tea drinker since she'd left Colombia, the dark brew tasted as bitter and foreign as the subject she had to broach. "I understand why you're grateful to him, but what I don't understand is why you told him what you did."

Renita stared at her impassively.

"You told him the child I had survived the birth. I saw the body, Renita. Amarilla showed it to me. The baby was dead."

Renita said nothing.

"I don't understand, *Tía*. Why would you lie to *Señor* Reyes? He should know the truth. The real truth." Maya glanced at Shepard and then looked away quickly. Shepard's sympathy had made their relationship subtly shift directions. The change disturbed her. She looked back at Renita. "You know the boy would have been his nephew."

Renita answered with silence once again.

"Renita, come on," Maya urged. "You have to explain this. You told *Señor* Reyes the child lived. Why did you lie to him?"

Maya's aunt glanced at Shepard, then she turned to Maya and said, "He's the one who lies."

CHAPTER NINE

SHEPARD HELD himself in check but barely. He should have known better than to trust the wife of Segundo Alvarez.

"Señora," he said softly. "You came to my office. You sat in front of me. You told me of Maya's child and then said that it lived. Are you denying you did all these things?"

"I went to you," she conceded. "But you must have mistaken my words."

Shepard's eyes met Maya's. In their depths he read a reflection of his own confusion, then he looked at Renita again. "The doctors at my clinic saved your child's life, *señora*. Surely you can not be so callous as to do this to me."

"I am not callous." Her spine perfectly straight, her words precise, Renita answered him...with another lie. "Your doctors did help my son...but that is all."

"You deny you came to me?"

"No. I came to thank you."

"And Maya's child?"

"He died."

Shepard drew a breath of frustration and Maya tried again. "Renita, *tía*…the first thing you said to me when I came to the door was that you were sorry. What are you sorry for?"

The older woman blinked rapidly but again, stayed silent.

Maya took one of her aunt's hands. The skin was rough and dry. "What's going on here, Renita? Tell me the truth."

"There is nothing to tell."

"Nothing to tell or nothing you *can* tell?"

With a flicker of fear, she glanced at Shepard then she pulled her fingers from Maya's, put her hands in her lap and blanked her expression. The visit was clearly over.

THE RIDE BACK to Bogota passed without Maya's notice. One minute she was stepping into the SUV and the next she was climbing out, her confusion rivaling her anger. Shepard had appeared as puzzled by Renita's disavowal as Maya, but had he been putting on an act? And if he had, to what end?

Maya continued to stew but as she shut the door of the SUV behind her, she accepted her agitation for what it was—a cover-up, a way to postpone facing her true reaction which was an immediate and overwhelming sadness. The idea that her child had lived, despite all her denials otherwise, had kindled a tiny flicker of impossible hope inside Maya's heart. Now that light had been extinguished and grief hovered nearby, waiting for her in the dark. All she could do was pray it would wait until she was alone to come out.

Shepard crossed in front of the vehicle and came to her side. "I intend to find out what's going on."

He might claim he was different from the rest of his family but Shepard shared at least one trait with them; they got whatever they wanted and he would do the same. Studying his face, Maya didn't doubt his determination.

But he was chasing a ghost.

"There's nothing *to* find out," she said quietly. "The baby died just as I said. For some reason we'll never know, Renita made up the story."

"She didn't make it all up. We saw the boy. And I have records that prove the child came to the clinic."

"That's fine but you don't have records that prove my child lived so does any of this really matter?" Exhaustion made her voice throaty and low. She rubbed her forehead then looked up at him. "All I care about right now is catching the next flight out of here."

"What about the truth?"

"I knew the truth before I got here. My child didn't live."

"You weren't *that* certain." His gaze etched its

way into her heart and his words followed. "Or you wouldn't have come down here."

"I had to make sure."

"Which means you weren't certain before."

She held up her hand. "I'm not going to argue semantics with you, Shepard. I'm wiped out—it was a horrible day and I'd just as soon forget about this whole thing." She started to step around him to head inside the villa, but he caught her arm.

"What about the photograph?"

"What about it?"

"I didn't send that to you, Maya, and it wasn't coincidental that you received it now. Doesn't that bother you?"

"Of course it does," she said. *It bothers me just as your hand on my arm does. Your touch is as dangerous, your dark eyes as frightening.* "But there's nothing I can do about that. There's no way to trace it. I tried the night before I left."

"Well, we need to try again. This is all connected, Maya. You can run back to Houston and pretend nothing's wrong, but you're still in danger. Someone knows your past." His lips thinned into a grim line. "The same someone who got to Renita."

The idea had passed through Maya's mind already. "You think somebody bought her off?"

"I'm *sure* something like that happened. They either paid her or threatened her to make her recant her story. They could have even said they'd harm her boy. When she opened that door and saw us, she was scared to death.''

''I don't know—''

''How else can you explain what happened?'' He tightened his fingers on her arm, another wave of awareness rippling over her at his touch.

''I can't,'' she stuttered. ''Not right now, but there has to be a logical reason.''

''There is,'' he said. ''And I just gave it to you.''

''You're wrong.''

''Then prove it to me.'' His eyes locked on hers. ''Find the grave and find the body. Then I might believe you.''

THE NEXT DAY'S FLIGHTS were booked. And so were those on the day after that. In fact, the first available seat Maya could get on a plane bound for Houston was at the end of the following week. Arguing with the ticket agent had done as much good as calling the other airlines. She'd come during tourist season and all the flights were full.

Lying in her bed that night, she listened to the macaws behind the villa, their wild cries the very sound that defined the country. With everything that had happened, she'd had little chance to think about what it meant to be back. Colombia was home, after all, and that meant something, whether she wanted to admit it or not.

Just as Shepard's argument had made sense, whether she wanted to acknowledge it or not.

There was no way she would return to Punto Perdido and look for her baby's grave, though. She couldn't. If she pursued this any more, the wounds she would open in the process might be fatal. Renita's bizarre behavior aside, Maya knew her baby had died, which was all that mattered.

She turned restlessly in the bed, the covers wrapping around her legs as she remembered Shepard's emotional support back in Punto Perdido. Without his help, she wasn't sure she would have had the strength and courage to continue. Being with Shepard made her feel stronger.

The thought sent her reeling and she told herself she was reacting to all the stress. Her life had been crazy before Shepard had even appeared, the judgeship occupying every moment of her brain.

Oh, yes, the judgeship.

She hadn't given it more than a fleeting thought since she'd left Houston. Her mind had been occupied with nothing but Shepard and the possibility he'd presented. That alone should tell her how much tension she was under.

Flopping over, she stared at the ceiling. How could she have set aside something she'd worked toward for years simply because he'd appeared in her office one day and told her what he had?

The answer, of course, was simple: A child's life

outweighed anything. But as important as that was, had more than that brought her here?

The question was a hard one because it was accompanied by a sensation she couldn't forget—the sensation of Shepard's hand against her arm. The simple touch had generated something it shouldn't have inside her—a longing to be held.

She shifted her gaze from the ceiling to the window. She'd tied back the heavy drapes and now a full moon poured silver through the glass. It seemed as if a thousand years had passed since she'd loved Renaldo. She'd had other men since then, one or two she'd even thought she could love. She'd chosen carefully and none of them had used her. But none of them had made her passion rise as he had and none of them had captured her thoughts so completely.

She closed her eyes and prayed Shepard couldn't, either.

SHEPARD EXPECTED NO ONE to be at the hospital when he finally went late that night. He'd purposefully waited so he could avoid the rest of his family but he'd also wanted to give himself time to think about the day's events. He was more worried than ever about the boy's safety, and Maya's, as well. He didn't know what to do about that, though. He didn't want her here yet he didn't want her to return to Houston, either.

The only other action Shepard could think to take was the one he'd mentioned to Maya but judging by her expression when he'd brought it up, he seriously doubted she'd look for the child's grave. It'd been an impulsive suggestion on his part and one he now regretted. Today had been traumatic enough for her and even though he didn't want to admit it, he felt sorry for her, the urge coming over him once more to pull her into his arms and console her any way he could.

The thought fled as Shepard neared his father's room and Javier stepped out unexpectedly. "Where have you been, baby brother? I expected to see you much earlier."

"I had things to do," Shepard said shortly, hiding his unhappiness to see Javier. Glancing through the open door to where Eduard lay, Shepard immediately saw that his father was better. He was resting comfortably, his breathing even and deep. He actually looked healthier than he had before the attack.

"Things to do?" Javier repeated. "That sounds interesting. Did these things involve the lovely Maya Velaquez?"

Javier's question brought Shepard's gaze back to his brother's face. "Actually, they did." He made his expression sheepish. "You know how that is…"

"She *is* a beautiful woman." Removing a cigar from his shirt pocket and unwrapping it, Javier nodded. "She hides her passion well, but something tells me you've seen it up close. Tell me the truth, *hermanito*. The business you have with *Señorita* Velaquez is not what we think it is, no?''

A coldness entered Shepard's bloodstream, its chill going deep.

''You have something else entirely on your mind.'' Javier struck a match on the nearby wall, just underneath the No Smoking sign. ''There's no work involved where she's concerned. I believe you brought her here to warm your bed.''

Javier touched the flame to the tip of his cigar and Shepard held out his hands in relief. The seed he'd planted in his brother's mind had taken root. ''You know me too well, Javier. I thought I could fool you, but I should have known better.''

''You could never deceive me, Shepard. You don't have the skill to do that.''

''Every Reyes has the skill to lie.''

''That's not what I'm talking about.'' Javier shook his head. ''You don't have the skill to think like me. And you need to remember that,'' he warned. ''It's going to be important one of these days.''

He drew deeply on the cigar then started down the hall. Halfway to the elevator, he stopped and pointed toward the room. ''They're releasing him tomorrow. He's been so horrible to the nurses, they want to get rid of him quickly.''

''Is it safe this soon?''

"The doctors say yes."

"Then there's nothing to do but bring him home."

Javier entered the lift, his not-so subtle threat disturbing Shepard more than it should. Shaking his head, he entered the hospital room and found his father awake.

"Where have you been?" Eduard demanded. "Javier needed you today and we couldn't find you."

"I had work to do." Shepard crossed the room to his father's bed. "I hear you're coming home tomorrow."

"I am," the old man confirmed. "And none too soon. They are killing me with their needles and their X-rays and their terrible food. A dog wouldn't eat what they put on the plate."

"That may be so, but you look well. Even better than before."

"Of course I do," he answered. "You would, too. I got away from your mother. I would never tell her so, but I believe she's poisoning me with all her herbal medicines. They're full of *la mierda!*"

"The tea she had you drinking smelled, I'll admit."

They talked a little longer of nothing important, then Shepard realized his father was tiring. He moved to pat the old man's shoulder. "I'll send the car early in the morning to bring you home."

His father nodded, his eyes closing as he gave his final orders. "Don't be late. I have things I have to do."

SHEPARD'S SISTER WALKED into the courtyard as he and Maya sat down to a late lunch the following day. Not knowing what to expect from Luisa, Maya tensed as Shepard greeted her.

Accepting his invitation to join them, Luisa pulled out a chair, then hesitated, her gaze shifting guiltily to Maya. "Do you mind if I eat with you?"

Maya held her hand toward the chair. "Of course, I don't mind, Luisa. This is your home, not mine. Please…sit down with us."

"I want you to know I'm sorry about the other night. I—I was way out of line and I'd like to apologize."

"There's no need for that. You were upset about your father. I'd feel the same."

"Maybe," Luisa answered, "but I have the feeling you'd keep it to yourself."

"Who's to say? When something happens to the people we love, nothing else seems to matter." She glanced down at her hands, remembering the grief that had finally overcome her last night, but only in her sleep. She'd woken to a wet pillow, her tears not yet dried on her cheeks. She lifted her eyes. "It's already forgotten."

"Thank you for being so gracious about it." Luisa's face lightened with relief and she sat down. Obviously, she'd regretted her outburst and wanted to make amends. She turned to her brother. "When were you planning to go to the mine? I'd like to take Maya to Teresa's."

Beneath the table, Shepard's hand captured Maya's wrist in a warning gesture. He squeezed her arm and answered at the same time. "I'm not sure yet. But why do you want to take her over there? Teresa is crazy."

"Don't say that." Luisa's defense was instant. "I love Teresa, and so does Mama. And her tea has helped Papá. That's why I'm going, actually. I need to pick up more. I wanted to get something for Maya, too." She turned to Maya. "It's my way of saying I'm sorry, but I thought you might need a break, too. All work and no play is not the Colombian way of doing business."

"I think our *hermano* knows that." Stepping through the nearest set of doors, Javier came to the table with a cup of coffee and a plate of fruit, taking the chair by Maya. He glanced in Luisa's direction and then at Shepard. "But I agree with you, Luisa." His gaze went to Maya and he spoke in a mocking voice. "Don't let our respectable brother keep you away from the dangerous santera. She might tell you all his secrets...."

Javier's words made Maya pause. Why would Shepard not want her to go to Teresa's? Maya couldn't imagine it had anything to do with the real reason she was here, but anything was possible, especially after yesterday. Remembering her thoughts about the woman at dinner the other night, Maya filed the questions away for later consideration. "I'd love to go," Maya answered, feeling Shepard's glower. "It sounds like fun."

"Then let me know which day you're going to the mine," Luisa said. "And I'll set it up."

Ten minutes later, Maya found herself alone again with Shepard. She started to ask him about the santera, but he took the conversation in a completely different direction.

"Did you think about what I said last night?"

"I thought about it but I'm not going back to Punto Perdido." She swallowed, her throat stinging from more tears. "I don't need to see the grave to know the truth."

"I understand," he said quietly.

"I've booked my flight home," she said. "Unfortunately I couldn't get a seat until the end of next week, Saturday after next to be exact."

A shadow crossed his face. Maya had no idea what might be behind it but she spoke quickly. "I'm going to get a hotel room, though. I insist. I don't want to burden you—"

"We've resolved that issue. It's better for you to stay here."

"But I don't want—"

Shepard stood up without warning, his eyes flinty in the cool air. "No hotel room. You will stay here."

She flared at his imperious tone but when she looked up at him, her response shifted to something more visceral. His eyes went past her for a second, then he bent down to her side and drew close. Her reaction deepened, her heart speeding up, her pulse racing.

"I'm sorry," he said softly, kneeling beside her chair. "I'm not trying to rule your life but you don't understand—" He cut off his words in midsentence, paused, then started again. "Look, today is Wednesday. How about we go to Muzo next week, say on Tuesday? That way you can visit Teresa, if you like, and relax a little. We'll spend some time at the mine then next weekend, you can fly out."

The words seemed stuck in her throat as he stared at her, their faces inches apart. "All right."

He didn't move, but his gaze did as it had before, going over her shoulder then coming back again. She wanted to ask him what he was doing, but his closeness had stolen her breath and she couldn't speak. He studied her face inch by inch, his look so heated and intense she could feel it, like fingers against her skin.

He edged toward her, and her breath caught somewhere in her chest. Slipping one hand behind her hair, he caressed her neck with a featherlight touch.

"There's one other thing," he said, his voice almost a whisper.

He raised his right hand and brushed her cheek then he dropped his fingers to the neckline of her blouse. They lingered there a moment too long then he brought them back to her face.

She found herself leaning toward him, imagining the feel of his lips as he kissed her. "Yes?" she whispered.

"My brother is watching from the window," he said. "Act as if you enjoy this."

HIS LIPS MET Maya's with the softest of touches and that's how he intended to end the kiss.

But it didn't quite work out that way.

Shepard held on to her instead, his hand tightening on the back of her head, his body responding with a heated rush of desire. Maya held steady for one long heartbeat, then she snaked her arms around his neck and pulled him closer.

Their kiss deepened, Shepard's mouth fitting so perfectly over Maya's, it felt as if they'd done this a thousand times before. The need to go farther suddenly threatened to push him over the edge.

Giving in as far as he dared, he let himself concentrate on Maya, on the press of her breasts against his chest, on her perfume as it enveloped them, on her hands where she held him. As her hoarse murmur rose between them and she parted her lips,

Shepard took advantage, his tongue flicking over hers. Her fingernails edged down his neck and then he was completely lost.

He forget Javier. He forgot Renaldo. Shepard forgot everything but the woman in his arms.

Maya was the one who realized Luisa had returned and was calling his name.

CHAPTER TEN

MAYA DREW BACK, and Shepard quickly stood, stepping behind her chair as if to protect her from prying eyes. Between her racing heart and thundering pulse, Maya had no idea how long it'd taken her to hear Shepard's sister but she'd obviously witnessed their encounter.

A moment later, she was gone.

Maya lifted her gaze to Shepard's face. He'd already composed himself but the satisfaction that lingered in his eyes bothered her.

"My father has arrived." His voice seemed different, too. Deeper, somehow. "Luisa wanted to let us know he was home."

"That's good." The moment felt ridiculous. She'd just experienced the most passionate kiss she'd had in years and they were making small talk as if nothing had happened. "He'll be more comfortable here, I'm sure."

"But you won't be." Shepard's dark eyes searched her face. "Not after that."

She didn't reply. She couldn't because she was too busy wondering how far they would have progressed had Luisa not appeared.

"I would say 'I'm sorry,' but I'm not." He smiled and she felt the ground beneath her shift. "My brother doesn't think you're here on business. After seeing us on the patio the other night, he took the situation a little further than I expected. Now he believes I brought you down here for the sole purpose of seduction. He was watching us from one of the windows upstairs."

Maya's senses were still reeling, but she managed to speak. "You encouraged him to think that."

"It's better than him knowing the truth."

"Why?"

"I explained that already—"

"You told me the news might disrupt the family. After meeting Javier, I'd say he definitely doesn't strike me as the kind of man who could easily be upset."

Shepard said nothing and she realized after a moment he wasn't going to. His words from before shot into her mind.

"It's not that simple."

"I need to check on my father, Maya." He started to walk away. "I'm sure you understand...."

"Actually, I do. More than you realize." Something in her voice must have alerted him and he stopped. Turning slowly, his gaze connected with hers as she stood.

"You're not worried about upsetting Javier," she said. "You'd rather him discount me as someone you want to sleep with than to give him any hint of the truth."

His silence confirmed her statement.

"Why is that, Shepard?" she asked softly. "What's going on? Why is it so important to you that Javier not know my connection to your family?"

His eyes became hooded. "I already told you you were better off not knowing the details. Leave it alone, Maya. It's not something you need to worry about."

Shepard went inside and she sat back down, her legs shaky and weak. He'd devastated her with a single kiss—the thought of what could happen in bed was one she couldn't even contemplate. But she proceeded to do just that. It'd been a very long time since she'd felt such complete and deep desire and she wasn't sure she wanted to now.

In fact, she felt suffocated by her reaction.

Because she didn't trust Shepard. Not for a minute. He was hiding something and she had no idea what.

WHEN SHE'D RECOVERED from Shepard's kiss, Maya headed straight upstairs. All she wanted was to close her eyes and let the narcotic of sleep slow her mind. Halfway down the corridor, she heard voices coming from one of the rooms that lined the hall. As she drew near, she couldn't resist peeking through the crack between the hinges and the door. Shepard's mother and sister were standing beside a stack of linens spread over a bed, Luisa holding the edge of a tablecloth, Marisol examining the crocheted lace that bordered it.

At first glance, Maya assumed they were discussing the state of the various items. Then Marisol's words drifted out into the corridor.

"She's not like us, Luisa. You have to remember that." Marisol clicked her tongue against the roof of her mouth to make a tsking sound. "If I'd known how crazy you were going to get over this, I would not have discussed the situation with you. She's not worth getting upset over. You're wasting your energy."

Marisol stopped all at once and jerked around, looking toward the open door. Maya had just enough time to duck away from the threshold and pretend she was walking by. A second later, Marisol stepped out of the room and into Maya's path, halting her progress. Maya sucked in her breath and put a hand to her chest. She didn't have to fake her shock. Her heart was racing inside her chest as if it wanted to flee on its own.

"*Señorita* Velaquez... Good afternoon. Was your lunch a good one?"

At the mention of lunch, everything clicked and Maya suddenly realized Luisa must have told Shepard's mother what she'd seen. They had been talking about Maya.

Or had they?

Marisol's expression was totally bland as she stared at Maya and waited for an answer, her voice smooth and pleasant.

"It was... very nice," Maya finally answered. She then changed the subject as rapidly as she could. "How is your husband? You must feel relieved that he's back."

"He will heal much quicker here. I don't trust the hospital—my herbal remedies will do what the doctors can not."

"You get them from Teresa, right? Luisa asked if I'd like to visit her."

"You should go and get to know her better. Teresa is a very special person." She inclined her head, an unreadable look crossing her face then disappearing swiftly. "Now, if you'll excuse me... Luisa and I were sorting some things. This is a large home and there's always work to do."

"Of course."

The older woman stepped back into the room. Then closed the door behind her. Firmly.

Maya continued on her way, the puzzling incident put behind her by the time she reached her room. She was getting paranoid. Marisol's dismissal was so smooth, they couldn't have been talking about her. And even if they were, what did it matter? Maya had too many other things on her mind to worry about—like the lingering feel of Shepard's lips against her own and the secrets he kept to himself— to give his mother's comments any more thought.

SHEPARD USUALLY WENT to the mines once a week, and if he wasn't there, then he worked from his office downtown. But with Maya in the house he didn't feel comfortable leaving. Using Eduard's illness for an excuse, he stayed close to the villa the next few days.

Which proved to be a big mistake.

Maya didn't venture far from her room, but she didn't need to. He could sense her presence in every room, her perfume lingering behind her, a word echoing after her. He told himself this heightened awareness meant nothing, but he lied. Their kiss on the patio, begun for Javier's benefit, had had repercussions. Shepard could no longer contain the thoughts he'd been suppressing because his conjectures had turned into reality. Now he *knew* what it felt like to have her arms around his neck, *knew* how soft her breasts were against his chest, *knew* how sweet her lips tasted pressed to his. He ordered himself to focus on his work and forget about her.

LUISA KNOCKED on Maya's door on Friday morning, her smile wide and bright. If the topic of the conversation Maya had overheard *had* been her, Luisa had clearly put it behind her. Maya decided she really must have misunderstood.

"I'm going to Teresa's this afternoon," Luisa said. "I know it's short notice, but can you come with me or are you heading out for the mine?"

Desperate to put aside the thoughts that were plaguing her, Maya accepted the invitation at once. "We're not visiting Muzo until Tuesday. I'd love to go with you to Teresa's."

They agreed to meet downstairs at three, Maya relieved to have something to distract herself. The thought Shepard had planted—of seeking her baby's grave—had begun to bother her again. How could she go home without being absolutely sure?

Almost as bad were the details about Shepard now lodged inside her brain. The warmth of his lips. The texture of his hair. The firmness of his body. The touch of his hands.

With hours to spare before her afternoon excursion, she called Patricia right after lunch, something she'd put off for too long already.

They chatted briefly about work and home, Maya asking about Franklin, Patricia asking about Shepard. Just as she'd done at Renita's house, Maya took more time than usual to get to her point. Finally, she didn't have a choice. They ran out of conversation and she could tell Patricia was getting impatient. She explained as quickly as she could.

"You're not coming back until next Saturday?" Patricia's voice filled with dismay. "Maya, we have work to do! The governor's coming and I—"

"I know, Patricia, but there's nothing I can do about this. The flights are full. It's tourist season here, coming and going. I didn't realize that until I arrived and now I'm stuck."

The silence that followed felt tense and accusing. Then Maya remembered her response to Luisa and Marisol's conversation. Was she overreacting again?

"I'm really sorry," she apologized. "After I return, I'll do the best I can to make up for lost time. I know how much the judgeship means to you and Franklin."

"What it means to…" Patricia repeated the words slowly. "What about what it means to you, Maya? You're the one who's going to wear that robe. Not us. How we feel about the situation is totally irrelevant."

"I understand, Patricia. I'm tired and my brain isn't working too well. I didn't mean that as it sounded. All I meant was…" Maya's explanation died out.

Patricia took a moment, then asked, "Was what?"

Standing by the desk in her suite, Maya turned to the window in front of her. The Andes loomed in the distance, green and mysterious. She swallowed. "I just meant that I understand how hard you've both worked to help me, Patricia. I understand I couldn't have gotten this far without your help. That's all."

Patricia's laugh sounded forced. "You had me going there for a minute, Maya. I thought you were saying something else entirely and I…got worried. This is not about me. It's about you. You're the one who'll be behind that bench. You and you alone. I hope you know that."

"Of course I do." Maya gripped the phone as she spoke. It'd always seemed obvious to her that she was filling shoes Patricia had never had the opportunity to wear. Had Maya made a leap in logic she'd shouldn't have?

"Well, I'm glad we're clear on that point," Patricia replied. "Being a judge is one tough job. You have to want it badly."

"And I do," Maya answered dutifully.

"Then we'll get it done," Patricia said with confidence. "But you have to get back as soon as you can."

"I booked the first flight I could."

"Well, I suppose everything works out for a reason. We'll see you soon, then."

Maya hung up the phone but her mind had already left the moment and jumped to Punto Perdido. Patricia's words, for some unknown reason, triggered the image of the midwife's house. Something about the young woman who'd come around the corner as Maya and Shepherd had passed had struck Maya as familiar but she hadn't been able to take the thought further. The girl was too young for Maya to have known yet she knew she'd seen her rounded face and braided hair before. Maya had been too upset to think about her any more, however. Until this very moment.

Everything works out for a reason....

Now she understood. It was all a matter of timing.

For eighteen years, Maya had lived with a ghost. The fact that her child had died had affected every aspect of her life. Like ripples in a lake when a rock is dropped, Maya's grief radiated outward to touch everything. If Renita had known something more, why hadn't she shared it? Her heart suddenly hammering, Maya picked up the telephone once again.

This time the arrangements took only a moment. This time she was more careful.

This time she'd be in Punto Perdido before Shepard even knew she was gone. And the truth would come out.

LUISA WAS WAITING for Maya when she came downstairs after lunch. They walked to her car—a dark Mercedes—then climbed in the back, Luisa making a face as she tilted her head toward the man behind the wheel. "I'm sorry about Hernando. I think it's pretentious to have a driver but unfortunately, it's also necessary. Kidnapping is a national pastime in Colombia. We can't go anywhere without a guard."

"Shepard doesn't take one."

Luisa arched her eyebrows. "Of course not—he's the mighty Shepard. He believes he's invincible."

"What about Javier?" Maya asked, her curiosity getting the better of her. "Does he think the same thing?"

"Yes. But for a much different reason." Her gaze filled with an emotion Maya couldn't read. "The men who'd want to harm us respect Shepard's power. They fear Javier's."

The big car made its way through the wealthy suburb where the Reyeses lived and into town. With each mile that passed, the scenery outside the tinted windows became less prosperous. The houses shrank as the number of people on the street swelled. Maya was surprised; she would have expected the *santera* to live in a posher neighborhood.

Sensing Maya's puzzlement, Luisa spoke. "Teresa won't move. She says her people live here and that's where she wants to be, as well. She needs to be close to them."

"Does she have a large following?"

"Oh, yes. She's one of the most well-known santeras in Bogota."

There had been many followers of Santeria in Maya's village but as a young woman, she'd paid scant attention. The faithful had depended on the potions and power of the santeros to heal them of everything. In Punto Perdido, love potions had been popular.

The driver slowed then turned down a side street. Two minutes later, he parked the car at the curb, directly in front of a small but neatly kept stuccoed home. Wooden boxes lined the two front windows and they held a riot of bright flowers in a hundred different shades. After the driver opened her door and Maya stepped from the car, she saw the wire cages beneath the planters. On one side of the front door, they held birds, chickens or doves, a parrot or two. On the other side, there were snakes.

Luisa knocked on the front door and Teresa

opened it immediately. She was dressed in white as she'd been the night Maya had met her. Smiling widely, she invited them both inside.

The house was surprisingly light and cheery, a faint lemony smell enveloping them as they entered. Maya wasn't sure what she'd expected but wide windows and hand-knit rugs hadn't been it. Teresa led them into a tiled living room and pointed to the sofa. "Have a seat, please. I just made tea. Let me go in the kitchen and get the tray."

Maya and Luisa sat down, a sense of calmness coming over Maya the likes of which she hadn't felt since Shepard had shown up at her office. Luisa began to chatter but Maya paid the woman little attention. She was too busy pondering her reaction. Teresa returned a moment later and handed them each a mug.

"You've left your weight at the door," she said approvingly as she sat down opposite Maya. "That's very good."

Maya's mouth dropped open. "How did you know—"

Teresa laughed and shook her head. "It's not magic, it's my home," she explained. "Everyone reacts to it the same way. They sit back and relax because that's how I've designed it. I want peacefulness in my life so I surround myself with things that promote that."

"Well, it certainly works," Maya admitted.

Luisa sipped from her tea. "You have Mama's All Heal?"

Teresa nodded to a small package on the table in front of them. "Right there. Tell her to be careful. She doesn't need too much in Eduard's tea, just a hint. I put something special for you in there, too. A little Sampson's Snake Root…"

Luisa blushed as Teresa turned and explained the herb to Maya. "You have to be careful when you use it but the results are almost guaranteed. It's for men—it helps them regain their sexual vigor."

Hiding her skepticism, Maya nodded with a serious expression.

"You don't believe me."

She started to deny the accusation but before she could speak, Teresa waved her off. "It doesn't matter," she said. "I'm not insulted."

Now it was Maya's turn to look embarrassed. "I'm sorry. It's not that I don't believe—"

"You don't have to explain," Teresa interrupted in a tranquil voice. "And you don't have to believe. The herbs will still work. That's why I included something for you, as well."

"You made her some perfume!" Luisa beamed. "Thank you, Teresa. I should have known you'd have it ready for us."

The woman in white smiled. "I did it last night.

I think you'll enjoy it,'' she said to Maya. ''Your essence was not an easy one to capture, though. You're a very complicated woman. You wear one face on the outside, but it hides another.''

Maya reacted politely but a faint uneasiness found its way inside her. ''We've hardly spoken. Are you sure you know me well enough to come to that conclusion?''

''Absolutely.'' Teresa spoke with confidence. ''And I don't mean to imply anything negative, either. You do what you do to protect yourself and that's perfectly understandable. In fact, there was nothing else you could have done to survive.''

Maya went still. Beside her she felt Luisa do the same. ''Is that true?'' Maya said stiffly.

''Oh, yes.'' Teresa answered the rhetorical question as if Maya had really meant it. Then she leaned closer. ''But you won't have to wear both masks much longer. Things have changed. You've already lost what you seek.''

Luisa's intake was audible but Maya's breath caught silently in her chest. She spoke sharply. ''What does that mean?''

''You know more about that than I,'' the santera answered. ''But what you don't know, is that you're going to find something even better. You need to use caution, though. I prepared a mixture of trefoil with vervain, dill and St. John's Wort that may help.''

Luisa leaned forward and asked the question Maya couldn't. ''What does the potion do, Teresa?''

Teresa looked at Luisa before her green eyes settled on Maya. ''It's a defense against evil. As long as your search continues, you and the people you love will be in danger.''

PLEADING A HEADACHE she didn't have, Maya escaped to her room the minute she and Luisa returned, saying she was going to skip dinner, as well. Luisa nodded. Teresa's pronouncements appeared to have left her rattled; she'd said little on the way back, and instead had stared vacantly out the window, her thoughts well-hidden. She said goodbye then went down the hall without another word. Watching her leave, Maya decided Luisa seemed friendly enough, but like her brother, she had secrets and Maya wondered what they were.

Putting her questions away, Maya stepped inside her room and went to her closet where she threw Teresa's bag of herbs to the bottom of her suitcase then locked it, shutting her mind just as tightly to the santera's vague words. Shepard had been right, Maya decided; the woman *was* disturbed. She had no idea what she was talking about. No other explanation made sense.

Turning her attention to the night ahead, Maya dressed early for bed in case anyone came by, then settled in for the evening with a copy of her favorite mystery writer's latest book. With the kind of discipline that had gotten her through law school, she held at bay all the troubling topics that wanted to intrude—the judgeship, her lost child, Shepard's kiss. When the mantel clock struck midnight, she dropped the book on the couch and walked to the window to stare out into the garden. She was still standing there when someone knocked lightly on her door. She opened it to find Shepard.

He was dressed impeccably, his hair slicked back and trimmed, his dark suit cut perfectly. Her heart bounced once, then again. She felt as if it landed in her throat.

"How are you feeling?"

His eyes held hers and wouldn't let go. He knew she was fine and had missed dinner so she wouldn't have to see him. She cursed him silently, which did no good at all.

"I'm fine," she answered. "It was just a headache. I took something and it went away. In fact, I was about to go…" To bed, she was about to say. Her words died, however, as Shepard closed the door and came into her room to sit down on the sofa. He was obviously going to stay for a while. She tried to maintain a cool attitude.

"Tell me about your visit to Teresa."

"It was entertaining," she said.

"Entertaining?" Repeating the word, he crossed his legs, propping his right ankle on his left knee before looking up at her. "Does that mean you don't want to discuss it?"

"There's nothing to tell," she said with a shrug.

His eyes were speculative, but he didn't pursue the issue. "Well, I'm sorry you missed dinner. It truly was entertaining…we had a dinner guest I think you would have enjoyed."

"I don't think they would have appreciated my attire for the evening." She picked at her sleeve then gestured toward his suit. "My robe might have been a little out of place."

His eyes went up and down her body. With a hem that reached the floor and a neckline at her throat, she'd thought herself well covered…until that point.

"Out of place for a formal gathering, perhaps." He tilted his head toward her fireplace. One of the maids had come in and started it while Maya had been in the other room. "But perfect for a casual evening by the fire with a glass of wine. Maybe you had the better idea…"

She pulled her robe closer then sat down in the chair beside the desk. It wasn't as comfortable as the sofa but she didn't want to get any closer to Shepard. "Who was your guest?"

He smiled as if he knew she was keeping her distance. "The Minister of Mines. My father hates him but he insisted on coming down for dinner just so he could goad the man."

Maya laughed in spite of herself. "Your father's quite a character. I'm glad he felt well enough to give the minister a hard time."

"Actually, I am, too," Shepard said. "The minister is not up to the task, but he's better than some we've had. He was no match for Papá, however. Even having just left the hospital."

"Why does your father dislike him?"

"Two reasons, the first of which makes him a complete idiot in my father's eyes: The man can't be bought."

She would never have expected Shepard to admit that the Reyes family controlled the mining ministry through bribery. "And the second?"

"He has made the mistake of agreeing with me on something. That alone is enough to qualify him for my father's enmity."

Shepard spoke easily but Maya caught the nuance behind his words. The family was not as tightly knit as Renaldo had led her to believe. Or Shepard was more of a maverick. "What is it you two agree on?" she asked.

"We'd both like better conditions for the miners,'' he said. ''More health care. Safer mines. Fair pay.''

She didn't bother to hide her surprise this time. ''That sentiment sounds more like Renaldo than you.''

''I suppose it does.'' He nodded thoughtfully. ''Renaldo and I shared more views than he knew. If he'd lived longer, he might have realized that, but our techniques to achieve those goals were too different for him to ever see the similarities.''

Instead of being awkward as Maya had anticipated, the conversation seemed to bond them in a strange way. Renaldo had been the curtain separating them; bringing his name out into the open pushed the divider aside.

''Do you miss him?'' she asked quietly.

''I did at first. When he walked into a room, the whole place would light up. There was something about him…''

''That drew people in.'' Their gazes met again. ''He *was* that kind of person.'' She stopped there, the rest of her thought staying silent. *But you are, too, Shepard, even more so than Renaldo ever was. You have a strength and intensity the power of which he would never have obtained.*

Shepard stood restlessly and crossed the room to stand beside the window. He spoke without turning, the fireplace sending flames to dance down his back.

"My mother and father loved him so much I thought they might die themselves when they found out he was gone."

Maya nodded, even though he wasn't looking at her. "He was killed before I left but I never knew the details. I read about it much later. In…a magazine, I believe." She thought of the report she'd ordered and all it had revealed. "He was foolish but he wasn't a coward. I never understood how he held that many soldiers off for as long as he did."

With a sharp pivot, Shepard turned to her, a strange expression coming over his features. "What do you mean?"

"I'm talking about the ambush. The…article explained how he was on his way back to *el despeje* to join his cadre when the Army troops caught him by surprise. There were quite a few of them, apparently."

"Renaldo wasn't ambushed by soldiers, Maya." His eyes flared into a darkness deeper than a newly dug grave. "That was just a story the governor put out for the press. I always thought you knew…."

She came to her feet without thinking. "What are you saying? That wasn't what happened?"

Shepard shook his head. "Renaldo wasn't caught by soldiers, Maya. Renaldo was murdered in cold blood."

AS IF NEEDING THE SUPPORT, Maya reached behind her for the back of her chair. She gripped the railing but just as quickly, she released it, grabbing Shepard's arm instead, her fingers digging into his flesh.

"Who killed him?" She didn't wait for Shepard's answer but continued, her questions suddenly flying at him so fast he got an inkling of how intimidating she could be in a courtroom setting. "Were there witnesses? When did this happen? Why didn't you tell me—"

Shepard gently pried her fingers from his arm and held them between his hands. He could tell she wasn't lying and the knowledge shook Shepard.

Maya had no idea her uncle had murdered Renaldo.

"I thought…you knew the truth," he said.

"I thought I did, too."

He led her to the couch where she sat down, her legs going out from beneath her. Shepard didn't want to look into her eyes because he knew what he would see. But he couldn't resist and when their gazes met again, he was unaccountably surprised…and then relieved, a wave of guilt quickly following. There was no love shining from her steady stare, no newfound grief, no unresolved emotions. She was shocked because she hadn't known, just as she'd said.

"Tell me the truth," she demanded. "Did you investigate?"

"Yes," he lied. This wasn't the moment to tell her about Segundo's part in the murder. "The national police came in at my father's insistence, but they found nothing."

"So whoever did it got away? No one was ever punished?"

"I didn't say that."

The color had come back into her cheeks but she still looked pale. Maybe because her eyes were so dark. "Explain yourself, please."

"There's nothing to explain. I've told you all I can."

"You told me nothing. And now you're lying."

"I've told you what matters. The person who killed Renaldo paid for his actions. Justice was done. I saw the proof."

She went stock-still, except for the pulse point at her temple that suddenly began to throb. "You killed him," she breathed. "You killed the man who killed Renaldo..."

"No. I did not kill him."

She studied his face, then understood. "But you know who did."

He didn't reply, the ominous quiet giving her the answer she needed.

"That's not justice, Shepard. That's murder."

He shrugged. "We have different names for things here in Colombia. You know that."

"And *you* know the difference between right and wrong. Vigilantism isn't the answer no matter where you live."

She was right, but that knowledge had made no difference. Once he'd known the truth, Eduard's grief and rage had consumed him, destroying what little respect for the law he'd had. He'd wanted the situation taken care of and that had been done. By the time Shepard had found out, it was too late to change the outcome, even if he'd wanted to. A muffled sound brought Shepard's attention back. Maya had moved away from him but the sudden trembling of her shoulders gave her emotions away.

He put his arm around her and forced her to turn. She resisted then gave in, blinking rapidly as she looked up at him. His heart fell as he saw her expression. He'd been fooling himself if he thought she no longer cared.

"I'm sorry I had to tell you this sad news," he said stiffly. "I would have done a better job had I known the circumstances."

"You don't understand."

"You loved my brother. What else is there to know?"

"I'm not crying for Renaldo. I'm crying for all the sadness. My parents, your brother, his killer, my child... How many people have to die before this will end?''

Shepard shook his head, unable to answer. He looked into her eyes, then lowered his head and kissed her.

HIS HANDS WERE WARM against her back, his solid steadiness a comfort. She allowed herself to absorb the strength she seemed to lack, then slowly but inevitably Shepard's kiss deepened and so did his intent. He was offering her solace, yes, but something else, as well. Something she suspected she needed even more.

Through her silk robe, she could feel the hardness of his chest against her breasts. She responded and kissed him back, her mouth opening to accept his tongue, every nerve in her body suddenly aware of what the moment held. This was for no one's benefit except their own and Shepard seemed determined she realize that. His palm slid down her spine slowly, as if memorizing each dip and curve and when it came to the roundness of her hip, he paused, his fingers tightening for a moment before moving on. She murmured in the back of her throat and his lips drifted to the edge of her jaw and then her neck. Her skin took on a heightened awareness and everywhere his mouth touched, she felt an individual flame ignite.

His hand came to the front of her robe and without her knowing exactly how, he had it unbuttoned. A moment later, he spread his palm over the swell of her chest just above her nipples. He kept it there for an eternity then slowly, inch by inch, he dropped his fingers until he held one breast. His lips followed, first to kiss, then to bite, then to suck.

In the dim corners of her consciousness, Maya heard her heart's faint warning. What were they doing? Where was this going? Was she crazy? The words were spoken in a language she didn't understand, however, the message of Shepard's tongue and hand much more clear.

She gave herself over to his attentions and silenced her better judgment. She was tired of thinking, tired of being confused, tired of the path her life had taken.

With a reckless search for something better, she closed her eyes and drew her hands through Shepard's thick, black hair, pulling his mouth back to hers for a kiss that quickly grew desperate. This was what she needed, she told herself. Not comfort. Not consolation. Not solace.

Just this.

CHAPTER ELEVEN

THE MOMENT SHE SURRENDERED, Maya felt Shepard pull away, breaking their intimate embrace to stare darkly into her eyes.

"This isn't right," he said, stepping away from her.

Maya wanted to grab him and bring him back, but he was already gone. Not just physically but mentally. He'd moved behind an invisible, yet impenetrable wall that Maya was well acquainted with—she was usually the one who hid there first.

"I can't do this," he said. "I can't take advantage of the situation. It's not right."

She trembled, but she kept her voice steady. "I'm a grown woman, Shepard. I don't let anyone manipulate me."

"You say that now, but how would you feel tomorrow?"

He clenched his hands tightly at his side and she realized that he was trying to keep himself from touching her again. If he didn't restrain himself, he'd be lost and for reasons she didn't understand, he couldn't have that happen. The warm flush of their encounter fled, leaving her heart cold.

"You came here for the truth, Maya." He flicked a hand toward the couch. "Not for this."

She lifted her chin, unable to think of any other way to defend herself. "I wasn't the one who started it."

His black eyes, so heated and compelling a few seconds before, filled with resolve so harsh she almost winced. "I understand. And I promise you it won't happen again. I won't be the second Reyes to seduce you and ruin your life."

SHE DIDN'T BOTHER to go to bed. After Shepard left, Maya locked the door and changed her clothes, slipping into the black jeans and turtleneck she'd already pulled from the closet. Stretching out on the couch, she let an hour pass and then another two, drifting in and out of a state too troubled to actually be called sleep. She was upset by the news of how Renaldo had really died, but Maya had still been aware that Shepard had not told her the complete truth. He was holding back something very important. She felt as if she were tottering on the edge of a steep and dangerous cliff.

Finally, after checking to make sure the lights in his wing were dark, she made her way down the stairs and to the kitchen. The day before she'd gotten "lost" and now she headed that way…to the service door she'd discovered that led outside. Ten minutes later, she found her waiting taxi. The driver accepted her extra cash and took her straight to the airport. She didn't breath easy until she was on the road heading out of town, the light of a false dawn leading her straight to the mountains, the battered engine of the SUV she'd rented, complaining as she gained altitude. Just as the sun broke over the Andes, she drove into Punto Perdido's square.

Stopping in the first café she came to, Maya ordered a double shot of *maté*. She needed all the liquid courage she could get for the task ahead. The herbal tea wasn't as powerful as the bottles behind the bar but she dismissed that idea. She needed her wits about her, too.

Draining the earthenware mug, she went back into the street. Within minutes, she stood in front of the midwife's house. The woman she'd seen the last time had just walked into the yard. She lifted her gaze to Maya's face, but this time her eyes widened.

Satisfaction swept over Maya as fear unmasked the girl's true age. Renita had told the girl who Maya was and that meant Maya was right.

She was looking at the midwife's daughter.

SHE TRIED TO RUN inside but Maya caught up with her. "*Por favor*… I need to talk to your mother and ask her some questions, that's all. I want to know—"

The girl looked over her shoulder, then up and down the street before meeting Maya's eyes. "My mother isn't here, and I can't help you."

She stepped back, as if to go into the house, but Maya grabbed her arm. "Would you ask her to meet me later?"

"She won't do that. She doesn't want to see you or talk to you."

Maya refused to give up. "Then maybe you can help me. Just answer a few questions for me, please. I'll pay," she added quickly. "I have money."

"No," she whispered, fear written over her features. "I can't talk to you." She looked around, then her eyes came back to Maya's face. "You must go away."

Maya had been prepared for resistance. Her fingers slid down the girl's arm and she pressed something into her hand. "Meet me at the cathedral. In the back. In ten minutes."

Her braids moved as the young woman shook her head again. Then she looked at the bill. Maya was sure it was more money than she'd seen at one time in her entire life. Her mouth was an O of disbelief.

"I'll be waiting," Maya said. "Meet me there and I'll give you twice this."

Walking quickly from the dirt packed yard, Maya turned left, avoiding the way she'd come. The girl's fear was contagious, and Maya wanted to make sure no one could follow her.

The village streets resembled a maze more than anything else. Maya darted into a nearby alley then ran down two blocks and cut back toward the square. Within minutes, she knew she was safe. Anyone unfamiliar with the small town would be hopelessly lost by now. After a few more twists, she was at the side door of the church. Taking a pew in the back, she settled in to wait.

The gilded interior hadn't changed. A tragic testimony to the sacrifice of the locals, the gold-leafed ceiling and walls gleamed richly in the dark. Under the watchful eyes of the painted saints, matching candlesticks and chalices weighed down the altar, their stems encrusted with deep green glints she knew were emeralds. Children had gone hungry to decorate this church, and Maya had been one of them. She closed her eyes to the disgrace. When she opened them, the midwife's daughter kneeled beside her.

"I shouldn't be here," she whispered. "My mother warned me you might come back."

"Why won't she talk to me?"

"It's too dangerous. Between the time that Renita

went to Bogota and you showed up here…well, things changed.''

Things changed? Maya's heart turned over. They'd been right—something or someone had gotten to Renita.

"What changed?" Maya demanded.

The girl shook her head. "I don't know. My mother wouldn't tell me.'' She lowered her face and crossed herself as a priest walked down the aisle and glanced toward them.

The man's black shadow vanished in the gloom and Maya spoke urgently. "Look, I'm not here to hurt anyone. I want to know the truth, that's all. Your mother delivered my baby eighteen years ago. She said it died but I've been told something different. Do you know anything about this?''

The girl's eyes darted to Maya's. They were round with fear and shock. "If it meant her own life, my mother would never harm a baby—''

"I'm not saying she did! But I don't know what happened that night. I saw the baby and I thought it was dead. It…it was blue and still—and they took it away. I was sick and then my family made me leave.'' Desperation filled her voice. "I have to know what happened!''

Her anguish seemed to touch the girl and her expression of reluctance faded into sympathy. "I'm sorry. I would help you if I could—''

Maya fumbled in her pocket, pulling out more bills. "Here," she said, forcing them into the girl's hands. "Just tell me what you know."

The girl shook her head and gave the money back to Maya. "I *can't* tell you anything," she said, her anxious words spilling out. "He'll come back and kill us all. He has people watching. They were here in the village the first time you came."

Maya's blood went cold. "Who are you talking about?"

The girl's eyes widened as she realized her mistake. She shook her head, glanced around the church once again, then sighed. "I don't know his name," she said softly. "He was just a man. A few days before you showed up, he was here. He went to my mother's farm and talked to her then after he left she told me I shouldn't talk to you if you came."

"What did he look like?"

"I didn't see him, but one of the girls in the field told me he was very tall with dark hair," she said. *"Muy guapo."*

Tall, dark and handsome. Shepard to a T, Maya thought with instant shock. He'd said Renaldo had told him she'd been from Mito and that he'd never heard of Punto Perdido, but that obviously couldn't be the case if he'd been here before...

The idea made no sense but she shouldn't be surprised. Nothing had made sense since she'd met Shepard.

"Was it the same man who was with me the other day?" Maya stared at the girl, willing her to answer. "You saw him with me, at the gate, remember?"

"I have no idea." She shrugged helplessly. "I don't know... I didn't see the other one."

Maya took a deep breath. "Did he threaten your mother?"

"He didn't have to," the girl said. "There was danger enough in his eyes. She knew without him saying."

"Why did he come to see her in the first place? What did he want?"

"My mother wouldn't say, but she was afraid of him, I could tell." The girl stopped and blinked. "If *mi gemelo* had been there, the man would have never gotten as far as he did."

"You have a twin brother?"

"I did, but—" She broke off abruptly. "Look, I have to leave, *señorita*. I have small children myself and I love them as my mother loves us. I'm sorry but I must go." She jumped up but Maya did the same, stopping her with a hand on her arm.

"I have to talk to your mother," she said, despair in her voice. "Please tell me where her farm is—"

"I can't." She shook her head then seemed to take pity once more on the crazy woman beside her.

"But it doesn't even matter…she's not there anyway. She had to go to another village and deliver a baby. She may not be back for days."

"But when she comes back—"

"She won't talk to you. It's not safe. The last thing my mother would do is bring harm to her family." She paused. "I'm sorry, *señorita*…but that's the truth and nothing will change it, not even your sorrow…."

The girl fled, the dark instantly swallowing her. A door sounded somewhere in the back of the church and Maya knew she was gone.

SHEPARD THOUGHT nothing of it when Maya didn't come down that morning. After last night's disaster he didn't blame her a bit; she had every right to be furious with him.

He was furious with himself.

He should have known better. Striding through the corridor to his father's room, he shook his head at his lack of control. Her inadvertent revelation that she knew nothing of her uncle's involvement in Renaldo's death had shocked Shepard, but it'd also freed him from a lot of the notions he'd held about Maya. That didn't mean he could now do what he pleased, though. Life didn't work that way.

As he knocked on his father's door then entered the bedroom, Shepard didn't think his life could get much more complicated. Then he neared his father's bed. The old man looked worse than ever. The skin hung from his face, and his eyes were deep within their sockets, dark and rimmed with shadows. Afraid to disturb him yet too worried to stay quiet, Shepard spoke softly. "Papá?"

Eduard lay still and pale for another moment, then his eyes fluttered open. "Shepard," he said hoarsely. "Is that you?"

Shepard leaned down and took his father's hand. "It's me," he answered, taking in the situation quickly. "You exhausted yourself last night, Papá. You shouldn't have come down to dinner."

"I had to," the old man answered. "I'm not going to let…that idiot ruin everything."

"The minister means well but I don't care about him right now. You need to get back to the hospital."

"No!" Eduard raised his fingers a few inches off the covers and batted the air above his bed. "Don't you dare take me back there! They'll kill me." He fumbled for Shepard's hand, found it and gripped it tightly. "Promise me!" he demanded. "Promise me you won't take me back there. I'll die if you do that to me."

Shepard looked into his father's burning eyes and knew he spoke the truth. The old man *would* die—

probably just to spite Shepard. "All right." He sighed. "But if you get worse…"

Eduard let go of Shepard's fingers with obvious relief. Before Shepard could finish his threat, he was asleep once more.

Shepard shook his head then looked at the table beside the bed. Anyone taking the amount of medicine Eduard consumed every day could hardly be expected to be alert. On top of everything, he'd obviously washed the pills down with a mug of Marisol's tea.

He lifted his father's hand, kissed it gently, then tucked it beneath the sheet. As he turned to leave, the bedroom door opened. His mother and sister stood on the threshold.

His mother spoke without preamble. *"Su amante ha corrido lejos."*

Shepard went cold. "Are you talking about Maya?"

Marisol nodded. "She didn't show up for breakfast or lunch. We went to her room just now, and it's empty."

"Maybe she's taking a walk. Did you check the patio? She could be out there—"

Marisol didn't let him finish. "She didn't sleep in her bed last night, Shepard. Her things are still there, but Maya is gone."

MAYA EMERGED from the darkness of the cathedral to the darkness of the square. While they'd been inside, a mountain of clouds had fallen out of the sky, shrouding the village with a mist so heavy it clung to her skin in droplets. She had no time to waste if she wanted to get back to Bogota before the weather got worse. But she had one more stop to make first.

Retracing her convoluted path, Maya hurried to her aunt's street. The instant she turned the corner, she knew she was too late. The place wore an air of abandonment, the boarded windows blank as dead eyes, the air above the chimney clean for once.

Renita and the boy were gone.

Disappointment swamped Maya. She went to the houses on either side and knocked but no one answered. She told herself she was being silly, but the neighborhood seemed frightened. There was nothing else she could do, except leave. She made her way back to the center of the village, and shivering in the damp chilliness, she sent a furtive look over the tiny park. The same shoeshine boys, the same beggars, the same old men sat where they'd been when she'd arrived.

Maya felt their stares as she walked quickly toward her SUV. Few outsiders came to Punto Perdido on purpose. Most who showed up were lost, and of those, very few were women. She reached the truck and climbed inside, thinking of how little she'd learned for her efforts. A tall, dark and handsome man had been in the village asking the midwife about Maya's baby. Was it Shepard? She didn't know. Had he found out anything? She didn't know. What should she do now?

She didn't know.

Maya put the SUV in gear and drove away, the unpaved roads outside the parking area already slick with mud and debris. By the time she neared the highway, she knew she was in for a rough return. The low clouds held lightning as well as rain, the brilliant flashes of electricity making it difficult to see. At the crossroad, she slowed to look for traffic, sent up a quick prayer then accelerated to pull out. The truck's rear tires began to slide, the heavy SUV listing suddenly to the right. Gripping the steering wheel with both hands, she fought the unfamiliar vehicle for control, finally managing to straighten it, her arms quivering from the effort. In the silence of the cab, she cursed soundly. She should have waited out the weather. On the winding road there were lots of places where someone could pull off and hide. Anyone could ram her vehicle and send the SUV off the side, killing her right there or dragging her into the mountains. She wouldn't be the first—or the last—secret hidden deep in these mountain passes.

The thought was frightening.

She slowed down and glanced in her rearview mirror. There was no traffic coming in either direction, but she constantly swept her gaze from the back to the front, checking frequently for headlights.

After an hour, she was still in the dark and alone. The rain continued to pound the metal roof of the truck but the lightning had begun to diminish. She didn't relax, however, until she had traveled more than halfway to Bogota. Taking a deep breath and easing her shoulders, Maya was on the second leg of a double switchback when something brushed her ankle.

Rental cars in South America didn't enjoy the same cleanup detail as their American counterparts. Debris was usually swept out when it reached the level of the seats, but in this case, Maya wasn't sure even that had been done. She'd hardly cared, though, when she'd taken the SUV. All she'd needed was transportation. The trash beneath the seat and the flies that came with it had been her last concern.

Sending a quick glance to the floor of the vehicle, Maya reached down to flick away whatever it was.

That's when she realized an empty paper cup was not what had touched her. It wasn't a crumpled newspaper or someone's misplaced map or a fast food container with a half-eaten hamburger inside.

It was a snake.

And it was huge.

She stared in horror then screamed as the animal began to wrap itself around her leg.

SHEPARD STOOD in the middle of Maya's bedroom. Even if his mother and sister hadn't said a word, he would have known Maya had left. The room felt void of life.

Shepard cursed angrily. He didn't want to consider the possibility that she hadn't left under her own power, but he knew that was an option. He'd hired private guards when they'd returned from Punto Perdido. They were supposed to be keeping track of her if she left the house. Assuming they were doing their job, he should hear from them, right?

Luisa spoke from the doorway. "What is going on?"

Shepard turned to face his sister, his suspicion suddenly heading in a much different direction. The apology she'd given to Maya the other day had bothered him; apologies weren't the Reyeses' way. "Why don't you tell me?"

"I haven't seen her since we came back from Teresa's. What makes you think I'd know where she is?"

Shepard stared in silence at his sister and after a few moments, her expression went from confusion to disbelief. He couldn't decide if the response was real or simply good acting. "You think I did something to her, don't you?"

"You made your feelings known."

Her eyes shifted nervously to one side before returning to his face. "That's ridiculous."

"Is it?"

"Of course it is! I can't believe you'd even consider such a thing."

"You were very angry, Luisa. More upset than a disagreement over a business situation would warrant. Are you sure there is not something else you'd like to discuss with me?"

She started to answer then stopped abruptly as Javier appeared beside her and their eyes met. Shepard told himself he was going nuts but he could have sworn some kind of communication took place between the two of them.

Javier turned his eyes to Shepard. "The office is looking for you. I told them I would find you and have you call them back."

Shepard nodded once then started out the door, pausing as he neared his sister. His eyes bored into hers. "We'll finish this discussion later."

"It's already finished," she said coldly.

Shepard gave her a look intended to tell her just how wrong she was, then he turned to hurry downstairs. A terrible feeling accompanied him that something bad was about to happen.

If it hadn't already.

CHAPTER TWELVE

MAYA TOLD HERSELF not to panic, but she was already past that point. Her scream reverberated inside the SUV and mixed with the sound of the rain pounding the roof. Gripping the steering wheel with both hands she kicked violently at the reptile with her other foot but the animal didn't budge. It had sought out her warmth and it wasn't letting go. Shaking her leg only seemed to make it more determined. Her foot began to tingle. Numbness would follow if she didn't act fast.

She steered to the side of the road, then slammed on the brakes. The truck responded by rocking and threatening to overturn. In the seconds that followed she decided the only thing worse than being trapped in a vehicle with a snake was being trapped in a vehicle with a snake and rolling off the side of the road. After the SUV settled into what felt like a deep rut, she realized she was repeating the same words over and over and over. ''Oh, God, please, oh, God, please, oh, God, please….''

She stopped and took a deep breath, then the vehicle shifted again, tilting at an impossible angle before shuddering into a final stillness. She sent her gaze to her leg.

The snake had moved up another inch. His diamond eyes stared at her with unblinking fascination. Her groan rasped in her throat. She knew nothing about snakes except this was the largest one she'd ever seen outside a zoo. The rough ride had dislodged the other end of it from underneath the seat and now she could see the whole creature. She immediately wanted to throw up. He had to be at least ten feet long, maybe more. Gray patches ran up and down his thick body, separated by dusky brown areas. On his side the light color paled and the dark went brighter, turning to a deep, rich red. She had no idea what kind of snake it was but his triangular head looked huge, close to the size of her palm. Two facts registered quickly.

One, the snake had a death grip on her leg.

And two, it hadn't climbed into her car on its own.

Both thoughts were equally frightening but at the moment all she could deal with was the first. Staying as still as she could, she glanced around the front seat of the vehicle for some kind of weapon. Her purse had opened and spilled when she'd driven onto the shoulder. A hairbrush, a tube of lipstick, a tiny flashlight—none of the items would do any kind of harm to the snake.

Getting out was her only option, and she had to do it before the snake could make its way any higher and trap her for good.

Inching her left hand toward the door, Maya tried to keep her movement slow and steady. Despite her best efforts, though, she caught his attention. The snake's eyes went to her hand, and then his tongue flicked nervously. At the other end, his tail whipped back and forth. A few seconds later—seconds that felt like a lifetime—her fingers found the cold metal latch.

She closed her eyes and said a prayer, then she eased down the handle and threw her shoulder against the door. The lock released—she heard the click—but the door didn't move; the weight of the listing vehicle was pushing against it. Maya screamed and hit the edge of the door again, this time with more force. It opened momentarily, a blast of cold wind and even colder rain slipping into the heated cab before the heavy door slammed shut.

The snake tightened its grip. She thought the cold would have made him loosen his hold, but that wasn't the case. For a heartbeat she wondered if she'd imagined the change and then she sucked in her breath, the faint memory of a *National Geographic* article coming to her. The story had been about snakes and how determined they were when hungry. Her heart stopped for two beats then shuddered inside her chest.

This animal hadn't come from beneath the seat because he was cold. He was hungry. And Maya was food.

Throwing her body against the door again, Maya grabbed the handle and pushed hard, fear renewing her strength. It opened a crack and more rain came in. She stuck her face into the downpour and a wellspring of energy rushed through her body and into her arms. She forced the opening wider and with inches to spare, she propelled herself out.

She crashed to the blacktop, the heavy door hitting her in the back as it closed.

A few dizzy moments passed as pain surged down her spine. Once again, she thought she might be sick but she choked down the urge and opened her eyes to look at her leg. She did throw up then.

The snake had come with her.

But only half of him had made it out the door...

"TALK FAST." Shepard cradled the phone between his ear and shoulder as he ran through the entry of the villa. "I'm on my way out and I don't have a lot of time."

His secretary complied. "The investigators you

hired followed the *señorita* early, early this morning. She rented an SUV at the airport then headed for the mountains but they lost her.''

Shepard spit out a curse as he opened the front door and strode toward his own vehicle. ''What do you mean, they lost her? How in the hell could they lose a woman in an SUV on a road no one travels?''

''They had a blowout,'' the woman explained. ''They saw her turn off the highway, but by the time they got the tire changed, she'd disappeared. They were near a road that went to a village called Punto—''

''—Perdido,'' Shepard supplied impatiently. He started his own SUV and wheeled it out of the courtyard, the guard barely getting the gate open before Shepard shot through it. ''What time did she leave the villa?''

''About four o'clock this morning.''

Shepard cursed again. Maya had been gone for over eight hours. Certainly long enough to get there and back if she'd been traveling anywhere else except Punto Perdido. The road to her village had become one of the favorites of the emerald bandits who roamed the countryside. Maya would be fair game, if not for them, then the FARC.

He ended the conversation abruptly and tossed the

phone to the seat beside him. Concentrating on his driving, Shepard sped toward the mountains.

WITH THE SNAKE DEAD, one problem had been re-solved, but Maya was now faced with an even big-ger challenge. The ruts the SUV had sunk into were deep and full of mud. The hubcaps were more than halfway covered, and she doubted she could get the vehicle out, even if she managed to get back inside. She walked to the rear of the truck but slowly. She'd taken a pretty good knock across the back—tomor-row the bruise would be nasty. Stepping into a patch of slick mud, she went down again. This time she managed to break her fall, but looking up at the truck from the ground, she quickly realized there was no way she could get inside.

The vehicle sat at a steep angle. The bottom of the door frame was chest level; she'd have to climb up the skirt, then grab the handle and swing over, just to reach the door. She remembered how heavy it'd been when she'd pushed it open. She'd had ter-ror to add to her strength then and it'd almost been impossible. Now she was hurt and the task would require even more force. She'd have to *pull* the door open instead of pushing it.

She couldn't do it.

For a moment, she considered trying the passen-ger side door but she gave up that idea instantly. The vehicle looked as if it might roll over. She couldn't chance being underneath it.

She crawled to the nearest tire then leaned against the wheel, stretching her legs out on the mudslicked pavement. There had to be something she could do.

There had to be.

She just didn't know what.

MAYA HAD NO IDEA how long she'd dozed. The rain had stopped, but her whole body felt sore and beat up. She moaned and tried to stand then found she couldn't. She'd stiffened in the cold and her movements were as tortured as her mind. She'd dreamed Teresa was hovering over her, her white dress billowing in the wind, her green eyes worried.

A rumble of thunder reverberated in the mountains behind her. Was the rain going to start again? She craned her neck to look but as the growl continued, she decided she wasn't hearing thunder. The deep thrum was coming from a vehicle.

Maya reached above her head and grabbed the wheel well, pulling herself up. She walked to the edge of the road and began to wave her arms at a speeding speck that had appeared in the distance. "C'mon," she pleaded. "You've got to stop, dammit, stop. You can't just drive by me."

As if it'd heard her plea, the whine of the engine began to change, the gears shifting lower. A Toyota Land Cruiser neared, a white one and fairly new, the windows tinted so dark she wondered how the driver could even see. Her heart picked up its pace as the

SUV slowed. A few minutes later, it rolled to a stop in front of Maya and the window facing her slid down silently.

Maya suddenly wished her prayer had gone unanswered.

From the front passenger side, a man stared at her with dead eyes. He wore a camouflage field cap and a black T-shirt and she could smell him from where she stood. He held a machete and his thumb played over the edge of it as he looked at her. Maya stayed where she was, but she couldn't stop her eyes from jumping past him. The vehicle held five other men and they all looked like him.

He tilted his head with the barest of nods and the doors flew open. In a heartbeat, the men surrounded her, automatic weapons in their hands.

He spoke, surprisingly in English, his voice as cold as his expression. "You have the trouble?"

"No," she said sharply. "Everything's just fine."

He raised a dark eyebrow and pointed the tip of his knife toward the ground. "Why are you out here in the rain with half of a dead snake beside your vehicle?"

When she didn't answer, he looked at one of the men behind her, and she heard the door to her SUV creak open. A rustle went through the group as they stepped back a second later. The man held up the other half of the snake. She lifted her eyes to the man in the truck and he confirmed her swift suspicion. Fear, hot and swift, stabbed her in the heart.

There were no good Samaritans in Colombia.

"That was a very good snake, *señorita*. It held much power and now you've killed it. My friends will not be happy."

She sucked in her breath, his meaning obvious. "Then let's call it even," she replied. "I wasn't too thrilled to find him inside my vehicle."

He said nothing and did nothing but suddenly the men closed around her. "You are coming with us," he said flatly. "Get inside."

Maya never had a chance to answer. The sound of an approaching vehicle broke the silence and this one was coming fast. Very fast.

The man nearest Maya grabbed her elbow in a rough grip, his fingers biting through her jacket. She tried to yank her arm away but he held on, dragging her toward the Toyota.

The brakes of the second vehicle began to squeal then Maya heard it stop, the man at her side going still as a ripple of nervousness made its way through the circle. Maya strained to see but her view was blocked. A door slammed and rapid footsteps came toward them.

All at once, the men in front of her parted, and she was finally able to see.

Relief stole her breath, but fear soon replaced it.

SPOTTING MAYA'S SLIGHT FORM at the center of the rebels, Shepard felt his anger almost explode. Two minutes more and she would have been gone, never to be seen again. Shepard's gut tightened at the thought.

The man in the truck greeted him laconically. *"Hola,* Sr. Reyes. *¿Qué tal?"*

Shepard repeated his question, his eyes narrowing dangerously despite the calmness of his demeanor. "What's happening? You tell me, Manuel. It looks as if you've been busy."

"Just doing our civic duty," he lied. "We saw the lady in distress and stopped to help."

Shepard knew he lied because Shepard knew the man. Manuel Santos was a lieutenant in one of the FARC's larger cadres and the only person he ever helped was himself. "What about your battles? Has Maldonado conquered so much you have nothing left to do but harass innocent women?"

Manuel Santos tensed as the name of his boss fell from Shepard's lips, his knuckles paling where he gripped the edge of the open window. "We were trying to give her aid," he said defensively. "Do you know her?"

"Yes, I do. She's a friend of mine. A very *close* friend."

Santos cut his eyes to the men and they stepped back. Shepard's anger *did* ignite then—Maya was filthy and clearly injured. He walked slowly to her side, wrapped an arm around her shoulder, then looked at Manuel Santos, his expression stony, his voice cold.

"You'll regret this, Santos."

The rebel blanched. "She was like that when we found her. We haven't touched her, I swear."

"Your words are worthless." His eyes locked on the other man's. "But mine aren't. If I were you, I'd watch my back."

Two minutes later, the men were gone, swallowed by the mountain mist.

Shepard turned to Maya, his hands on her shoulders. She laid her head against his chest and that's when he realized she was trembling. An urge came over him to chase Santos down and beat him into a bloody mess. "Maya…"

He could feel her take a shaky breath and then she lifted her head. "They never touched me. I'm fine…"

Shepard's curse escaped before he could stop it. "You wouldn't have been fine for long."

"How did you know where I was?"

He didn't answer and a spark of resentment came into her eyes when she realized what that meant. He'd had her followed. Her reaction didn't last, though, because it couldn't, considering the outcome.

"Why did you return to Punto Perdido, Maya? I thought you'd accepted what Renita told us."

"I did." Her gaze slipped away from his, then returned. "But then… I don't know. I just had to go back, Shepard. To make sure, that's all."

"And are you sure now?"

"I don't think I'll ever be sure." Her voice quivered.

"What happened?"

"Renita is gone."

He wasn't surprised but there was more. He could tell by the way she'd spoken. "And?" he prompted.

"And…that's it."

She was lying as surely as Santos had been, but Shepard didn't press her. Now wasn't the time.

He tilted his head toward her vehicle. "Where'd the snake come from?"

She shuddered lightly. "It was in the SUV. It— it climbed up my leg and that's when I drove off the side of the road. The man in the Toyota as much as admitted he'd put it in the cab."

Shepard stepped to the body of the snake and studied it closer. "This is a red-tailed boa." He nudged it with his boot. "They're usually pretty docile."

"Well, someone forgot to tell him that. He seemed determined to make me a meal."

"How did you kill him?"

"I just wanted to get away but he came out of the truck with me and the door fell on him...after it hit me." She touched her back gingerly.

The silence between them stretched into a tension-filled moment. Shepard wanted to chastise her but what good would that do? Maya Vega was an independent woman who went her own way, and if he hadn't realized that before, he definitely did now. Despite the trouble that generated, he found himself admiring her guts. Not too many women could have held Santos at bay, even for five minutes.

"Thank you for helping me," she said quietly.

He lifted her chin until their eyes met and then he dropped his fingers. "You can thank me better by remembering this..." He paused. "Everything—and everyone—in Colombia is dangerous. Even when you think you're safe, you aren't."

THEY RETURNED to Bogota in Shepard's SUV, leaving the rented vehicle by the side of the road. In a voice that left no room for discussion, Shepard told Maya it would be taken care of and she didn't need to worry about it.

For once, she found herself grateful for the way he took charge. And not just for the vehicle, either. She couldn't let herself think about how things might have turned out if he hadn't shown up when he did. Not now, not here, with him only a foot away from her.

"I'll call the doctor when we get to the villa, but in the meantime take one of these." He reached into the console between them and brought out a small pill bottle. "I hurt my leg at the mine earlier this year and the doctor gave them to me. It's ibuprofen, extra strength."

She shook a couple into her hand as he pulled a small flask from beneath his seat and passed it to her. She looked at the bottle of brandy and raised one eyebrow.

"You can't take them dry," he said. "It's all I have."

After what she'd just gone through, the point seemed ridiculous. She washed the pills down with a stinging shot of the liquor and a flame flared inside her. She realized—when she stopped—that she'd been shivering, from fear or cold, she didn't know which.

"I don't need a doctor," she said. "I'll be okay."

He shot her an exasperated look. "Why do you insist on rejecting my assistance?"

"I'm accustomed to taking care of myself. I have since I was a kid."

"Well, you needed my help with Santos," he pointed out. "Or did I misread that situation?"

"I *did* need your help and I'm very appreciative

of it. But generally speaking, I can take care of myself. That's all I meant." She touched her scraped skin and bit back a groan. "It's all right," she said from behind gritted teeth. "Really."

But by the time they reached the villa she wondered how she was going to make it from the car to the house. The combination of ibuprofen and brandy had left her more comfortable, but she didn't know if that was because it'd actually helped the pain or because she now no longer cared.

The question fled her woozy mind when Shepard drove to the rear of the house, stopping before a small side door. He parked the car and looked over at her. "You're staying in my guest room tonight."

Her pulse took an extra beat. "Why is that?"

"I don't want to disturb the rest of the household. It'll be easier if the doctor comes back here."

His excuse was so blatantly false it seemed pointless to challenge him. Did he suspect she'd learned about his own visit to Punto Perdido while she'd been there? Was she going to disappear tonight? He'd said himself people vanished all the time in Colombia and no one ever noticed.

She told herself she was being ridiculous and suddenly it seemed impossible to dredge up the effort she would need to protest the arrangement. The next thing she knew Shepard was carrying her inside.

CHAPTER THIRTEEN

THE DOCTOR CAME and went, leaving advice and salve, saying all Maya needed was time and rest. His nurse helped Maya clean up, then got her settled in bed and bandaged her scrape, massaging the doctor's cream into her stiffening muscles. The minute they were gone, Maya went to sleep.

Shepard stared at her still form, then stepped outside to his patio and phoned his mother. Maya had headed out of town into the mountains toward Facatativa and Zipaquira, he lied. She'd wanted to see the Salt Cathedral and *los Piedras de Tunja,* but she'd gotten lost then had a minor accident. Reassuring Marisol that Maya was fine, Shepard cut off the rest of her questions and hung up. He then made two more calls.

He spoke quietly and listened more than he talked. When he had finished both conversations, his suspicions were no longer suspicions.

They had become facts.

WHEN MAYA WOKE UP, she shifted in the bed, the stiffness in her body instantly reminding her of everything that had happened. Easing from the covers, she touched her back, glancing at a nearby clock. She wasn't sure which surprised her more; the fact that she'd slept so long—it was almost 2:00 a.m.— or the fact that she actually felt much better than she would have expected. She crossed the room and looked out the window.

Shepard was on the patio, and as she stared, he raised a hand and beckoned for her to join him, pointing toward a door at her left. For reasons she didn't want to examine, she hesitated, then, as she'd known she would, she opened the door and stepped outside.

He closed the gap between them, his footsteps bringing them together, his eyes drawing her in even more.

"How are you feeling?" he asked. "Are you in any pain?"

"I'm a little sore," she admitted, "but no pain. What kind of salve did that doctor give me? He could make a fortune back home with it."

Shepard laughed lightly and Maya realized it was the first time she'd ever heard him genuinely amused. The sound made her wonder about all the other things she didn't know.

"It wasn't the doctor's cream that made you feel better. It was my brandy." He tilted his head toward a small table. In the darkness a silver tray gleamed, a bottle and three glasses resting on top of it. "Let me get you some more."

Setting down his tumbler, he poured her a drink before she could refuse. She took the glass and looked up at him. Their fingers brushing, Maya held her breath as a ripple went down her back. When the feeling had passed, she slowly exhaled.

If Shepard noticed, he gave no indication. His demeanor returned to its usual intensity as he sipped from his glass then spoke, his voice grim. "I contacted some people. I know where the snake came from and I know how it got in your SUV. Santos told the truth. He did it." He smiled oddly and another shiver tripped along her spine, this one from fear. "He won't be doing anything like that again. He won't be doing much of anything anymore."

"Why did he do it? He doesn't know me—"

"He was paid."

"By whom?"

Shepard's eyes shifted to the house. Then he looked back at her and lied. "I'm still working on that answer."

Placing her drink on the table, she set about getting her answer another way. "Maybe I can help you figure it out," she said slowly. "While I was in Punto Perdido I learned you were right about Renita.

Before we arrived, a man *had* been in the village, asking questions.''

''Who was he?''

She held his eyes with hers. She didn't really believe it had been Shepard—that didn't make sense—but dammit it to hell, he *was* hiding something. ''All I know is that it was a man…tall and dark. *'Muy guapo…'*''

His expression stayed unreadable.

''The midwife's daughter told me 'something had changed' between the time Renita came to your office and we went to Punto Perdido. That's why Renita wouldn't talk to us that day.'' Her voice was a hoarse whisper. ''It had become too dangerous. What does that mean?''

''I don't know.''

''Who do you think he was?''

''I can't say.''

She lifted her hands to his chest and looked up at him. ''Can't or won't?''

''Let me handle this, Maya.''

''I'm a grown-up. I can take care of my own problems.''

He took her hands, but then dropped them, stepping back from her with an angry curse. ''I'm trying to keep you alive, Maya. The more you know, the less chance I'll have to reach that goal. Leave it alone.''

"But you're the one who came to me in the first place! If you'd never shown up, I wouldn't even be here."

He froze beside her, his eyes as cold as the Andes snow. "I'm well aware of that fact, Maya. It's one of the main reasons I don't sleep at night."

His admission made her heart stumble. She met his stare head-on and the growing desire she'd been fighting gained a foothold deep inside her.

"What's the other reason you can't sleep?"

He placed his hands on her shoulders, his dark gaze never leaving her face, his accent deepening in a way she hadn't heard before. "You are."

SHEPARD HAD NO MEMORY of how they got to his bedroom. All he was conscious of was Maya. The way she looked, the way she smelled, the way she felt...

Stopping in front of the bed, he eased her down and slipped his shirt from her shoulders, his touch far more urgent than it should be. He wanted to be gentle and take his time, to make her want him as badly as he wanted her, but the moment they acknowledged their desire his body ignited with a passion that quickly grew out of control.

A passion that Maya shared.

Helping him shed his own clothing, she kissed him over and over, her fingers hungrily tracing lines against his skin. Her caress was urgent and greedy and he reveled in it.

The window beside the bed was open but the cool night air did nothing to chill the fever between them. Shepard returned her kisses, his tongue parting her lips insistently, his hands sweeping over the curves of her body. She was soft and pliant yet he was more aware than ever of her underlying strength. Like the past she fought to conceal, Maya had denied her passion with fervor. Now the need had a power all its own.

When he lifted his mouth from hers and pressed it to her neck, she moaned in protest but the sound faded as his lips moved over her body. Unconsciously she followed his action, her tongue rasping over the pulse point at the bottom of his throat, her hands dipping between them as she grasped him tightly and began to stroke him.

He lost himself in the pleasure of her touch, his hands going to her breasts. They were as round and full as he'd thought they'd be. He bent his head and kissed her gently. Her skin tasted sweet, he thought in a daze, the scent rising from her body fragrant and compelling. Lifting his lips from one nipple he went to the other and found it the same. His fingers trailed over the rest of her body and then he pulled himself away from her, moving his mouth lower, her body quivering beneath his heated tongue until she cried out and made him stop.

Rolling to the side, he reached into his nightstand for a condom. A moment later, he brought Maya to him, his hands behind her hips as he lifted her above him. She gasped then clutched his shoulders as he slid inside her and began to move.

When her moan shattered the silence between them, the sound released a tightness deep inside Shepard that he hadn't even realized he'd been holding in. With a final push, his own desire climaxed, the heat of the encounter vaporizing any regrets he might have had. If this woman had belonged to his brother, nothing they'd shared could have come close to this, and that was a fact Shepard knew he would never doubt.

A second later, Maya shuddered again, then collapsed against his chest. He held her tightly and wished time would stop.

MAYA WOKE as daylight eased through the shutters and crept into the room. Shepard lay beside her, sleeping peacefully, his forehead clear, for once, of worry and concern. She turned over in the bed and propped her head against one hand to study him. She ought to have regrets, she told herself. What they'd done would complicate matters even more, but she couldn't feel remorse. Their lovemaking had gone beyond the physical to fill an emptiness she hadn't acknowledged until Shepard's arms had gone around her. She felt complete again, the connection they'd made returning something she'd been missing for a very long time.

The revelation puzzled her. How could she feel this way about him, knowing who he was?

The answer came swiftly.

He had a strength of character few others even dreamed of. He was kind and strong and powerful in ways she'd given up thinking even existed anymore. He wanted to protect her and everyone else that he cared about, including her son, if he was even alive. The discovery triggered a series of revelations.

Shepard was a good man. A good man she could love.

Because of his last name, she'd made assumptions she shouldn't have. She'd been blinded by her past but now her eyes were open. The danger Shepard posed was not to her life, but to her heart.

WHEN SHEPARD WOKE the second time, Maya was gone.

He grabbed his robe and hurried into the hall. As he passed the bath, he heard running water and feeling foolish, he shook his head. Maya wasn't going to put up with any kind of overprotectiveness. He'd better learn to calm himself.

But how could he, knowing what he did?

Going to his kitchen, he fixed a pot of *café con leche* then carried the tray and mugs outside, the coffee leaving a fragrant trail behind him.

Maya appeared in the doorway just as he filled the second cup. She wore one of his shirts and nothing else, her dark hair hanging in wet tendrils around the oval of her face. "I need the clothes from my room," she said.

He came to where she stood and cradled her head between his hands. Kissing her deeply, he eased his thumbs along the line of her neck. He'd had her suitcase brought to his room while she'd slept, but he didn't say so. Her skin was still wet from her shower and all he could think about was carrying her back to bed and licking the drops with his tongue.

"Why do you need clothes?" he teased. "They'll get in the way and we'll just waste time taking them off again."

"Do you plan to keep me hostage here? Naked and in chains?"

"That sounds like a good plan to me."

She stepped back and held the plackets of his shirt. "Maybe it does," she said carefully, "...and maybe it doesn't."

Shepard had never experienced a moment that seemed to last forever, but this one did.

"I'm not sure we should have done what we did," she said slowly.

"Because of Renaldo?"

"Renaldo and everything else. The person who wants me gone… Our different lives…" She lifted her gaze. "What kind of future could we possibly share?"

"Do we need to look that far ahead?"

"I'm not into casual flings."

"Neither am I, Maya. What happened between us last night was not a fling, nor was there anything casual about it. I don't operate that way."

"Then what happens next?"

"What happens next is…what happens next. We don't have to plan it out. Let's focus on something we can control, which is how to keep you safe."

"That's easy," she said. "I'll go back to the States."

"What makes you think that will help?"

"I was fine there until…"

"Until I arrived," he supplied grimly, "and the photograph came." He shook his head. "Going back to Houston is not the answer, Maya. Not now. You're better off where I can protect you."

At his words, her expression shifted subtly. He'd confirmed something for her, but what?

She took a moment to compose herself, then spoke quietly. ''It's not just me, is it? I should have caught on sooner but I didn't get it until this morning. I was right...''

''What are you talking about?''

''There are others besides my son and me you want to protect.''

He could lie, he told himself, but sometime, somewhere, the lies had to stop.

''Who is it, Shepard? Is it Luisa? Your mother? Javier? I know you're protecting someone so don't try to convince me you aren't. Just tell me who it is.''

He opened his mouth to reply, then the door to the patio swung open to reveal Javier on the threshold.

CHAPTER FOURTEEN

JAVIER'S GAZE RAKED over Maya's body then Shepard stepped forward, putting himself between Maya and his brother. "We have doors for a reason, *mi hermano*. They're there so you can knock."

Shepard's words were ignored. "The *picando's* been moved up. It's taking place today."

"Why has the day changed? I thought we agreed on the end of the month—"

Javier shrugged. "Esteban did it. Ask him if you have a problem."

Shepard cursed then turned to Maya. "Once a month, we let some of the men harvest stones from the tailings. We keep *las gangas en bruto*—the better ones—but what's left goes into the miners' pockets. It's their most important benefit. I have to be there to manage it."

"But Shepard—"

"I'll take care of the *señorita* for you." Javier's eyes returned to Maya, making her think of the snake that had been in her car. His stare held the same predatory coldness she'd seen in the reptile. "We haven't had a chance to talk about the store. This would be a good time for that discussion, no?"

"No." Shepard answered for her. "That will have to wait for another time. I'll take care of *Señorita* Velaquez." When he spoke again, Shepard's voice was even colder. "Was there anything else you needed, Javier?"

"That's it." Javier's expression regained its usual laconic slackness. "You do what you want." He looked at Maya and tipped his cigar at her. "Another time, perhaps?"

Maya echoed his words, her face a mask. "Another time, perhaps…"

He left after that, the wrought iron gate slamming behind him. Maya watched the metal shiver for a moment, then she followed Shepard inside the house. She entered the bedroom in time to see him dialing his cell phone.

The conversation was quick and when he hung up, his voice was aggravated. "Javier was telling the truth. I'll have to go up there."

He came to her side and brought his fingers to her face. The caress was brief but Maya needed nothing more for her desire to swell again.

She took his hand and pressed it to her cheek before reluctantly releasing it. "I understand," she said. "But you can't leave me here without answering my question first. Who are you protecting, Shepard? I have to know.''

"This is not the time to explain, Maya. When we get back tonight, we'll discuss it.''

She started to protest but he cut her off with a look so full of resolution she found herself stepping back. The closeness they'd shared the previous night was gone without a heartbeat's notice.

He pointed to the foot of the bed. ''Your suitcase is over there. Dress warmly. You're coming with me to the mine.''

THEY MADE IT to the airfield in record time. Shepard wheeled his SUV into the restricted parking area behind the airport's main terminal and headed directly for the helipad, sending Maya a quick glance. He felt bad about the way he'd put off her question but he had to be absolutely sure.

Unfortunately, he was getting closer and closer to that point. He'd had Javier's phone records checked. His brother had called Miguel Santos the day before Maya had gone to Punto Perdido. Javier had hired the FARC thug to put the snake in her car and then to follow her.

Javier knew Maya's true identity.

The knowledge brought regret. Holding Maya in his arms last night, Shepard had come to understand how much she meant to him. She was a very special person…someone he could be content with forever. If she'd been with his brother, if she'd belonged to FARC, if she'd lied to him or not…Shepard didn't care. He loved her.

But that love would go no further. Maya was too smart to fall for another Reyes. Once she knew the real story, anything they might have shared would be destroyed.

The pilot started the helicopter as they stepped from the SUV. With Shepard's arm around Maya's shoulders they ran through the wash of the blades and jumped inside. Airborne a moment later, they headed north and into the mountains, Bogota dropping away behind them, danger waiting ahead.

MAYA HAD NEVER SEEN anything like it.

As they flew over the enormous black pit that was the Muzo mine, she stared in amazement at the teeming activity below. The ground itself seemed alive, men working with picks and shovels, hoses snaking in all directions, guards standing around the perimeter. She pressed her face against the glass and peered through a soft mist.

Over the chopper's noise, Shepard explained the confusion. "We mine the bare ground and in open tunnels. The deposits are in veins of calcite that run through the shale. That's the black powder you see everywhere."

The pilot made a second turn and dropped in altitude, the details becoming more apparent.

"That's one of the shafts right there." Shepard pointed below them.

She followed his finger. Men were hauling buckets up and down from a dark hole, carrying the full ones from the mine to men sitting at tables situated in a series of open-air buildings.

"Those are the sorting sheds." He tapped the glass. "The men look at the deposits and do a preliminary sort. Later the rough material will be graded again for color and clarity and a cut is determined." He glanced at her and she read his love for the mine in his expression. "Muzo stones are special. I could look at a gem that's hundreds of years old and tell you if it came from there. They have very unique inclusions and color. The matrix and crystal forms are found nowhere else."

Sending her attention back to the mine and away from him, he nodded toward the ground again. "See the dozers? They handle the surface work."

Lined up like hungry predators, dozens of bulldozers waited at the top of the promontory, a series of terraced steps beneath them leading deep into the earth. One by one, they lumbered out to scrape the topsoil and vegetation away. A second later, they pulled back. The men then swarmed the exposed shale, attacking it with tools or sticks. Mud covered everything.

Shepard tapped the pilot on his shoulder. "Put me down at the guard shack, then take the *señorita* to the office and wait there." He sent his gaze to Maya's. "You'll be safe there. We shouldn't be too long."

The helicopter immediately dropped, Maya's stomach following. Shepard jumped out as they touched down, then she and the pilot were back in the air. Moments later, they descended again, this time to a concrete pad beside a series of plain stuccoed buildings.

The pilot pointed out the office and Maya stepped from the helicopter.

The air was heavy and wet, and she got the impression it was always like that. Pulling her jacket closer, she headed for the office.

She'd barely made the first step when the door opened.

"Maya!" Luisa said. "Javier called and said you were coming." She smiled brightly. "I'm so glad you're here!" She looked behind Maya. "Where's my brother?"

Maya answered as she entered, Luisa closing the door behind them. "We dropped him off at the pit. He wanted to check on some things before they started the *picando*."

"Oh, you should have stayed to watch! It's fascinating, really. Are you sure you don't want to go back?"

"I don't think Shepard would like that," Maya replied. "He was pretty determined to do it his way."

Luisa seemed to accept Maya's answer, albeit reluctantly and turning around, she led Maya to the back of the building. As Maya followed, something about Shepard's sister struck her as different. When Luisa turned right and entered a small office Maya realized what it was. Instead of her usual glamorous outfits Luisa wore jeans and a denim shirt. Her face was free of makeup and her hair was pulled back. She looked much younger.

Luisa's appearance was not what really caught Maya's attention, though. It was her attitude. She seemed hyper, her eyes too bright, her words coming fast. Maya suddenly remembered the day Eduard had been taken to the hospital. Did Shepard's sister use drugs? They entered a room that was plain and unadorned, a spot where work was done and nothing else.

"I'm not interrupting your work, am I?" Maya asked.

"No, not at all. I'm glad you could come." Sitting down behind a green metal desk, Luisa pointed to a thermos. Two cups sat beside it, one half full. "Would you like some tea?"

She'd had nothing to eat or drink all morning. "I'd love some," Maya replied gratefully. Taking the chair in front of Luisa's desk, she reached for the aluminum container and filled the clean cup. As she drank, Luisa picked up her own mug then swiveled to the radio set behind her when it filled the room with a sudden staccato conversation.

She replied quickly, clicking off the microphone and turning back to Maya with an apologetic look. "There's always something going on," she said. "But I like it that way. I'd rather be busy than bored."

Maya took another sip. "I understand. Frankly I'm surprised you aren't in charge of part of the operation. You and Shepard seem much more involved than..." She broke off abruptly, realizing what she was about to say.

Luisa drained her mug and reached for the thermos. "Much more involved than...Javier? We are but Papá wanted him in charge."

She refilled her cup then held it in her hands, looking out the office's single window. It was set high, almost to the ceiling, and bars covered it, inside and out.

Her curiosity getting the best of her, Maya asked

the question she'd been wondering since she'd arrived. "So why *is* Javier in charge?"

Luisa brought her eyes back to where Maya sat. She answered simply, waving her free hand to the office and the mine outside. "My father didn't want to change his will, but he wanted to reward Javier because he took care of a problem. This is what he received."

"It must have been some problem," Maya said over the rim of her mug.

"It was." Luisa lifted her eyes to Maya's. "Javier tracked down the man who killed our brother, Renaldo. He slit his throat, then sent him to Hell. He was a peasant named Segundo Alvarez."

SHEPARD STARED at his head of security. Rio Gamez had been with the family for years and Shepard trusted him without exception.

"I'm sorry, Shepard, but I had no idea you didn't want to hold the *picando* today. Javier said change it so I changed it."

Javier had said Esteban had changed the date, now Rio was saying Javier had ordered the switch. What was going on? Shepard didn't know, but he instantly felt uneasy.

Pulling a hard hat down from one of the pegs near the door, he put aside his reaction. "It doesn't mat-

ter one way or the other. I'm not going to let down
the men. We'll do it now.''

They left the shack that served as Rio's office and
started walking to the edge of the open pit. Every
hundred yards a guard stood, cradling his automatic
weapon and looking down at the miners. A huge
security force worked at Muzo but some stones still
left the mine illegally. Others were washed into the
nearby waterways along with the tailings. The
downstream *guaqueros,* or treasure hunters, fought
violently over these scraps, four or five dying every
week in disputes of some kind.

Through the light rain, Shepard strode past the
guards. Ten minutes later, he was at the newest face.
Even the mist couldn't hold down the black dust that
swirled as the men dug steadily through the exposed
calcite vein. On a ridge behind them, the dozers
idled, each driver waiting for the boss's signal to
scrape more earth.

The supervisor looked up as Shepard approached
and the men began to yell. With *El Jefe* in the pit,
they knew the scramble would soon begin.

Rio began to organize the group. Participation in
the event was a reward given to selected miners,
sometimes for hard work, sometimes for turning in
stones that could have fed their families for the rest
of their lives. The mining operation shut down while

these lucky men lined up. Shepard watched, but his thoughts returned to his brother.

Javier had wanted Shepard out of the villa. He'd known changing the date of the *picando* was the best way of achieving that. Why? Did he want to get to Maya? Had he found the boy?

The air split with the signal to begin, Shepard's questions going on hold. He focused on the one bull-dozer still running and nodded. The engine rumbled into a throaty growl and the machine crawled toward the step just to Shepard's left. The blade lifted slowly then bit into the wall of limestone. The min-ute the machine stopped and the tailings had fallen, the chosen men were given the signal, while the rest stood by. They surged forward in a wild wave and with frantic determination, began to hack and cut through the now loose stone, some with sticks, some with shovels. There was always violence in the pit— it hovered over the mine like a cloud—but on this day, the men's energy was directed toward the earth and not each other.

The craziness lasted until the supervisor blew his whistle. The men fell back from the leavings and Shepard stepped forward to inspect what they'd found. He made his way quickly down the line, se-lecting some of the promising chunks, but letting the men keep more than he usually did. He was at the end of the line when one of the miners reached into his dirty, beat-up bucket and held out a hunk of black stone.

Because of the mud and shale, all Shepard could see of the man's face were his teeth and the whites of his eyes. Still, he recognized the old-timer. He'd been *un guaquero,* one of the more successful ones, and hearing of his way with the stones, Shepard had hired him to work inside the mine, instead of out. Shepard automatically smiled at the man, then he took the rock.

Embedded in the center was a raw emerald the size of a small grape. Not huge by any means, the stone would lose a good portion of its weight when polished, but Shepard immediately knew it was special. He spit on the face of it, then rubbed it against the sleeve of his shirt. Staring deep into the rough, Shepard felt the magic of the stone. He was instantly captured as he imagined how great it would look dangling from a gold chain nestled between Maya's breasts. His fist closed around the rock and he lifted his eyes to the man before him.

"Well done, *amigo.* You keep what else is in the bucket and next time, you get a head start." He slapped the man on the back and the other miners cheered, the noise of their enthusiasm rocking the terraced pit. They were tough men, but Shepard knew how to gain their loyalty. With the right mix of reward and control, he'd managed them for years.

The celebrating continued as Shepard waved to the men then rejoined Rio and the cut supervisor to stand on the fringes. He watched for a few more minutes before turning around and heading back.

He'd taken half a dozen steps when he realized the men's voices had changed. The ones at the far end of the tailings had begun to scream, this time in horror. His gut rolled inside out and he turned.

Chaos had broken out. The line of miners he'd stood beside seconds before were fleeing in panic, tumbling over each other in their haste to get away. Shepard tried to make sense out of the pandemonium but he couldn't see. The stampede had changed the normal swirling dust and dirt into a black fog that obliterated all sight.

Suddenly the *guaquero* who'd found Maya's stone stepped out of the dark tornado. His terrified eyes found Shepard's, and he screamed a warning as he grabbed Shepard's shirt and flung him to one side.

A second later, the mudslide caught up with them, the bulldozer right behind it.

MAYA STARED at Luisa, her mouth dropping open. "Did you say Segundo Alvarez?"

"Yes."

Maya was glad she was already sitting down. Her head began to spin, a dizzy feeling washing over her. She set her mug of tea on Luisa's desk. "Segundo Alvarez was my uncle."

"I know." Luisa's dark eyes gleamed as she stared back at Maya.

"But how…" Maya stumbled over the words, all her verbal skills failing her. "How do you know he killed Renaldo?"

"Javier told us. My brother has done many things of which I do not approve, but this is not one of them. He had a duty and he did it."

"I don't believe this…." Maya looked across the desk, her mouth suddenly dry despite the tea, her heart slamming against her chest as her earlier bout of light-headedness returned with a vengeance. She struggled to stay calm.

"Don't bother to act surprised." Luisa came from behind the desk.

"I know nothing about this."

"You're lying." Luisa paused as if considering her next move. "But if you want to persist with the pretense, I'll go along."

"It's not a pretense! I don't know what you're talking about."

"Then I'll spell it out for you. We hadn't heard from Renaldo in months because he'd gone into hiding. His cadre's location had been revealed to the Army and he'd barely escaped. Your uncle contacted our family and said he could arrange a meeting with Renaldo. We were thrilled. But what we didn't know was that Alvarez had not only turned in Renaldo's men, he'd kidnapped Renaldo. He didn't have information. He had my brother and he wanted money in return.'' She took in a deep breath and let it out slowly, her angry words coming with it. ''Your uncle killed Renaldo just as Javier arrived. Javier killed him in return.''

The room tilted and Maya's stomach heaved, her heart stopping then starting again. Her uncle had killed Renaldo? Before she could say a word, the radio behind the desk crackled loudly, the harsh static that emerged startling her into silence. A panic-filled voice flooded the office.

''Bring the chopper back! *¡Venga rápidamente!* There's been an accident on the side of the mountain. *El Jefe* needs help!''

CHAPTER FIFTEEN

DASHING BENEATH the twirling rotors, Maya jumped into the helicopter right behind Luisa, barely making it inside as the struts left the ground. She wanted to ask Luisa more about her awful news, but as they descended into the giant bowl of black dust and confusion, a sweep of vertigo hit her hard. She gulped and waited for her equilibrium to return. When it finally did, she grabbed Luisa's arm and started to speak. Her words were swallowed as Luisa gasped and shook off her grip, pointing instead to the ground below.

The entire lip of one of the cuts had collapsed and a swell of mud had moved down the slope, taking men, equipment and everything else in its path with it.

All thoughts of the past fled instantly. Maya held back a scream but barely. Shepard was down there somewhere!

Maya searched the rubble with unblinking eyes. Had he been hurt? Was he buried beneath the mud and debris? Her heart raced, the beats coming erratically as she tried to pray for Shepard. The words wouldn't come. She was too scared.

The chopper landed with a bone-rattling jolt. Maya felt for the door handle but her fingers were trembling too much to open it. The pilot reached past her and threw the latch.

Luisa jumped out first. Before Maya could follow, a ghost appeared out of the mist, a man's form cradled in his arms. Others were beside him, trying to help, but the mud and the rain had turned every movement into a parody of motion. Maya's breath stilled. Whoever he was, he wasn't moving and from the limpness of his arm, she doubted he would again.

The man who carried the body leapt into the chopper and laid his burden on Maya's feet. The helicopter rose immediately, leaving Luisa and the others behind.

They were high in the air and over the nearest mountain before Maya saw that the man at her feet wasn't Shepard.

OVER THE ROAR of the engines, Shepard tried to explain, his face covered in black dust, his features totally obscured. "One of the dozers went off the side of the terrace. It started a mudslide then plowed through the men." He ripped off his jacket and wrapped it around the miner's head. Blood continued to flow. "Get me a blanket," he instructed Maya. "There should be two behind the seat."

She jumped up quickly. Too quickly. She almost fell, catching herself at the last moment. She shook her head, then she edged toward the rear and rummaged through the storage bins at the rear of the helicopter. She grabbed a blue wool lap rug. When she came back to his side, her face was pale, her skin clammy.

"I—I thought it was you," she said. "I thought you were the one who'd been hurt."

Shepard raised his gaze from the injured miner and their eyes met, a connection even stronger than their desire building between them. All at once, he realized just how much he loved Maya, the conviction so strong, it shocked him. Now was not the time, but when this was over, he'd have to make her understand…somehow.

Putting his emotions aside, he squeezed her hand and took the blanket, tearing it into another bandage.

"Was he trapped?" she asked.

"He fell beneath the dozer."

Maya sucked in her breath. "Oh, my God, Shepard. If this *had* been you…"

He finished the sentence for her. "…I'd be ten feet under that mudslide right now. He pushed me out of the way and saved my life. Because I saw where he went down, we were able to get him out fast.''

Her skin took on a sudden green tinge as Maya closed her eyes then reopened them. ''You're a lucky man.'' Her voice shook.

''That depends on how you look at it.'' He glanced at the bleeding man then brought his eyes back to hers. She looked ill but when he told her his news, she'd feel even worse.

''Someone started that mudslide on purpose, Maya. The dozer's wheel was locked and it was headed straight for me.''

THEY WERE AT THE HOSPITAL in twenty minutes. The miner was unloaded and whisked off to the emergency room the second they landed. More dizzy and confused than ever, Maya fell behind as Shepard grabbed the doctor.

''He saved my life, Doctor. Please…you have to save his.''

The man promised to do his best then he ran through a set of swinging doors to follow his patient. Shepard began to rage, his curses ringing down the hospital corridor. Maya had never seen him like this, but his words barely registered. She melted into a nearby chair, her shortness of breath returning.

After a moment, she pushed back the spinning walls and looked at Shepard. Her body and mind felt disconnected. The first confused and out of control, the second sharper than ever, more focused than when she stood before a jury. "Why didn't you tell me Segundo killed Renaldo?" she asked without warning. "Luisa...Luisa told me everything. Why didn't you tell me what you knew?"

He took the chair beside her. From the look on his face, she could tell he was surprised, but there was more than just that in his reaction.

The words were clear in her brain, but Maya's tongue was thick as she spoke. "You should have told me, Shepard. I could...could have handled the truth."

"I don't know what Luisa told you, but it wasn't the truth because she doesn't know it. She and my parents believe your uncle killed Renaldo, but I've never been sure. When Renita came to me, I knew it was time to investigate and either confirm my suspicions or put them away once and for all."

"You had doubts...so you used me—and the possibility of my son—to find out more?"

"Yes, I did," he said softly. "But after I met you—and I got to know you—the situation changed. I knew then that you had no idea of Segundo's involvement. Everything was already in motion by that point, though, and I couldn't stop the inevitable."

A heavy weight pressed down on her chest. Something was wrong with her—physically wrong—but she persisted. "And what was 'the inevitable'?"

"Someone else found out about you. I thought it was Javier. He's the one who sent you the photo, he had the snake put in your car, he told Santos to kidnap you. But could I be wrong? If Luisa knows, too…"

Maya stayed silent, a wave of confusion rolling over her. "Why do they want me gone?"

"Money," Shepard answered flatly. "Renaldo was the favorite son and he would have inherited the controlling interest in the mine had he lived. When your uncle kidnapped him, the situation played right into Javier's hands. He got rid of Renaldo, then murdered Segundo to cover his tracks."

Despite her growing illness, Maya's training kicked in without conscious effort. "But Renaldo's portion would have automatically reverted to the estate."

"Not in this case. My father had his will written so that Renaldo's *heirs* would inherit his part."

She touched the gold cross at her neck and beneath her fingers, her pulse jumped, then slowed… then jumped again. Her mind wandered crazily.

Shepard gave voice to what she couldn't. "If he's

alive, your son stands to gain a fortune. But if he's dead—''

''—or never found—'' she added.

Shepard nodded. ''His portion reverts to the estate.''

''And all of Eduard's children get slices from a bigger pie.'' Maya felt her face blanch and without thinking, she leaned away from Shepard.

Suddenly, she remembered what she'd told him when they'd first met...

''There is no one truth.''

A few hours before Maya had thought she was falling in love with Shepard. He'd kissed her and made love to her and she'd let him know all her secrets. She'd made one tragic error, though.

She'd forgotten who he was.

Behind Shepard, the lights in the hallway shimmered. Maya put her hand on the edge of the chair to steady herself. ''All your father's children would get a larger portion. *All of them.* That includes you, Shepard. You're a Reyes, too.''

MAYA'S WORDS STRUCK HIM with the force of a well-aimed hammer, the blow landing right on his heart.

''I love you, Maya. You're more important to me than anything else, including that fact.''

Her eyes widened and she pulled in a sharp

breath. "You've picked a strange time to tell me so."

"Perhaps this isn't the best place—" he nodded toward the hospital corridor "—or the best time, but I'm telling you the truth. I realized it in the helicopter on the way over. I thought you felt the same way."

Gripping the arms of her chair, she looked away from him and didn't answer.

He took her chin in his hands. "Maya?"

"You threatened to expose my background."

"I had to find out the truth."

"You lied to me."

"Only by omission."

"You used me."

"Because there was no other way. I was trying to protect you and, if he was alive, your son," he said. "I wanted to keep him safe, Maya. But when we met, everything got more complicated."

Her stare looked strangely vacant. "I should have known...."

He started to speak, but she cut off his words. "You're a Reyes. You do what you have to to get what you want. Blood *always* tells."

She shook her head then stood up, her face now totally void of color. Shepard stared at her in shock, seeing all at once what he'd missed before. Her pale, clammy skin. The dilated eyes. Her confusion. He took a step toward her but he was too late.

She crumpled to the floor.

SHEPARD DROPPED TO THE TILE, one hand going to the base of Maya's throat, his other slipping behind her head to cushion it. Her skin felt cold and slick, but what worried him even more was her pulse. He couldn't find it.

He began to shout for help, but two nurses were already coming toward him. They slid to a stop then pushed him away, their hands replacing his own.

In less than a second, the one nearest Shepard looked up in panic. "Go to the station and grab a doctor!" she ordered. "Hurry! She's not breathing!"

Shepard ran down the hall, yelling. Doors opened as his cry was heard and the hall came alive with help.

All Shepard could do was stand back and watch.

Five seconds later, they'd cut off her blouse and a doctor was pounding on her chest. From down the hallway, a rumble sounded and he looked up. Three nurses frantically wheeled a cart around the corner, almost crashing before they righted it and continued, even faster, to Maya's prone body.

The crowd around her parted momentarily then swelled again. Each nurse and doctor seemed to grab a different item off the cart and began to do something to it. From his place against the wall, Shepard finally understood.

Maya's heart had stopped and they were trying to restart it.

CONFUSED AND IN PAIN, Maya lay on the floor. She wanted to scream but before she could do anything, her eyes were drawn to a lone figure a few steps away. It was Shepard, his face gray with fright, his eyes full of fear. His hands were clasped before him as if in prayer, the impotence he felt obvious in his agonized expression.

One of the doctors yelled for everyone to step back. Maya didn't understand what was happening to her until it was too late.

The doctor flattened two black paddles against her chest. The power behind them shot into her body.

A searing flash of light started in the center of her chest then spread out in tendrils, wrapping itself around her nerves and muscles, even invading her blood. In the blink of time it took for the blinding sensation to travel from her heart to her feet, her brain registered the unexpected image of a man. The shadow-like figure wavered then stilled and she realized it was Renaldo. Or was it? Something seemed different about him but she couldn't tell what.

She started toward him but instead of beckoning

to her as she would have expected, he held up his palm and stopped her. His lips didn't move, yet she heard him speak.

"The baby needs you."

The vision shimmered once then faded.

A surge of energy raced over Maya's body and went straight into her heart. She gasped as her lungs screamed for air, the pieces of the puzzle tumbling into place, Renaldo's message making everything clear. She had a son, a son who lived and needed her.

She couldn't die.

Not now.

THEY SAID HE COULD see her but just for a minute.

He told them he'd stay as long as he wanted.

But five minutes after Shepard entered Maya's hospital room he was grateful when the nurse tapped on the door and made him leave. He couldn't have handled much more.

Pale as a winter sky, Maya lay perfectly still under Shepard's gaze, her only movement coming when she breathed, her chest rising up and down in time to the machine beside her bed. Her skin gleamed, and someone had brushed her hair and fanned it over the pillow. She looked as if she had died.

And she had. The doctors had refused to let her

go, however, and under their frantic ministrations, she'd come back to life.

Shepard tried to catch his breath, but he wasn't sure he could. The past few hours had been a nightmare. When would it end? *How* would it end?

He forced his feet to move and he headed down the hall where Marisol had been since shortly after he'd called home. All he'd told her was that he needed to find Javier and Luisa. His mother had said they were both gone. Luisa was at the mine and Javier had left for Panama. An unexpected trip, she explained, that had come up right after Shepard had gone to Muzo.

Sitting in one of the plastic chairs that lined the waiting room's walls, Marisol raised her gaze as Shepard entered. She looked ill herself, dark circles beneath her eyes, violet shadows in her cheeks. She stood up slowly, her expression worried, every one of her years on her face. "How is she, Shepard? Did you get to see her? Will she be all right?"

"I haven't been able to talk to the doctor yet. All I did was step inside her room. Have you heard from Javier or Luisa?"

"No." She shook her head. "No one knows anything about either one of them."

Turning away, Shepard went to the coffee machine in one corner of the room. He wanted nothing to drink. He'd had four cups of the vile concoction since they'd brought Maya up, but he had to do something with his hands, his face…his heart… He picked up another cup then mindlessly added sugar and milk.

When he finished, his mother was beside him. "Is she going to live, Shepard?"

"I don't know. And I doubt the doctors do, either." His voice went hard. "I swear to God, I'm going to kill Javier. He wanted both of us gone! He's behind all this!"

Her eyes filled. "You don't know that for certain, Shepard. And even if he managed to start that mudslide, how can you blame Maya's problem on him? You said her heart stopped!"

"It did," he answered. "But they don't know why. I'm willing to bet—"

"No one has to bet anything. We know why."

Shepard pivoted quickly, coffee sloshing from his cup. The doctor stood in the doorway of the waiting room.

"Tell me," Shepard commanded.

The man sank into the nearest chair and motioned for Shepard to join him. "Come sit down, my friend," he said, his weary eyes meeting Shepard's. "I don't think you're going to like my explanation."

Marisol immediately crossed the room and took the chair next to the man.

"I'll stand," Shepard answered, his chest going tight. "Just tell me she's going to live."

"I can do that," the doctor replied. "She *will* recover."

Relief washed over Shepard, taking the strength from his legs. He followed the doctor's advice at that point, sitting down in the chair opposite the man. *"Gracias a Dios…"*

"You'd better thank God," the physician said. "Because it is a miracle. If she'd been anywhere else when this happened, you'd be planning her funeral right now." He rubbed his forehead in a gesture of exhaustion then dropped his hand. "The damage to her heart would have been fatal."

"Did she have a heart attack?"

The doctor shook his head at Marisol's anxious question. "Not exactly. Her heart stopped beating—as it would during a heart attack—but not of its own accord. Something stopped it for her." The doctor turned to Shepard. "I realized this when her bloodwork came back from the lab. Her electrolytes were off the scale. They were completely *locos…*"

"What does that mean?" Marisol held her hands in her lap. She was squeezing them so hard, her knuckles had gone white.

"There's a very complicated answer I could give you, but in the end, it doesn't matter. The simple truth is this—the young lady had enough poison in her body to kill two men. The adrenaline in her system helped dull the effects, but she won over death because she wanted to. She fought like *el tigre* and for that reason, she has won.''

Shepard went still, cold disbelief holding him in one place. ''Poison? What kind of poison?''

''The kind I don't know about,'' he confessed with a grimace. ''The test results were inconclusive. All I know is the end result. This couldn't have been an accident. Someone tried to kill your friend, *Señor* Reyes and *that* is why she almost died.''

CHAPTER SIXTEEN

THERE WAS LITTLE MORE the doctor could say, and finally, Shepard had to let him go. The lab was trying to isolate the substance that had caused Maya's heart to stop, but at this point, they didn't have a clue what it might have been.

The doctor left Shepard and Marisol sitting in stunned silence.

Marisol was the first to speak. "This is all my fault." She stood up slowly and put a hand on Shepard's shoulder, her eyes brimming with guilt. "I'm responsible for this, *mi hijo*. If Maya dies, her blood is on my hands."

Ice replaced Shepard's bones. "What are you saying?"

"I know who Maya really is, Shepard. I've known about her for years."

She nodded at his shock. "I'd almost managed to convince myself she no longer existed, but then you found her and brought her home. I wasn't sure why, but I suspect I know." Her eyes went soft. "You found out about the baby, didn't you?"

Shepard came to his feet. "You knew about the baby?"

"I heard the rumors, yes. But that's all they were. Just rumors. I looked for years, Shepard. The baby did not survive or I would have found him." She touched his cheek then dropped her hand. "Why did you start searching for him anyway?"

"I was told he lived."

Her eyes rounded. "By whom?"

"That's not important," he answered impatiently. "I want to know why didn't you tell me of Maya."

"I told your sister," she said, "and that was a big enough mistake for me. I didn't plan on repeating it."

"And Javier?"

"Javier has no part in this." Marisol shook her head and looked at him in pity. "It had to be Luisa. She must have gotten something from Teresa. Her herbs are very powerful, and her spells the same."

"Don't give me that nonsense—"

"It's not nonsense!" Marisol flared. "Teresa has a thousand different ways of killing people, you fool! Don't you think Luisa would know that? She could have stolen something from Teresa without her knowledge."

The sudden image of a red-tailed boa hit him. "You should have warned me," he said bitterly. "I might have been able to prevent this."

"You're right. I should have. But I was too worried about your father to think of anyone else." She looked away from Shepard and spoke quietly. "It had to be Luisa. She's always wanted the mine for Vincente. I told her there was no child, but she understands a mother's determination. She knew as long as Maya was here, the search would continue."

"Does Javier know who Maya is?"

"I have no idea, but if he did, it wouldn't matter. Your brother would never harm an innocent person. He's an honorable man."

A door closed inside Shepard's heart. How could she be so blind? "You call a murderer an honorable man?"

"That happened a long time ago, and he was simply carrying out his father's wishes. It was what he had to do."

"'What he had to do?'" Shepard repeated the excuse without thinking, his outrage getting the best of him. "Javier did what he wanted to, Mother. And you've never known the half of it."

"I know what I need to."

Did she know what had really happened the night Renaldo had died? Did she know the truth Shepard had always suspected but had never been able to prove? His mother stood before him with a spine like a rod, her eyes two black coals.

If she did know, she'd never tell Shepard.

And if she didn't know, he couldn't tell her.

He left the room without another word.

IN THE LATE AFTERNOON, groggy but alive, Maya came to on her own. The tubes had been removed from her throat and only an IV line remained.

There were guards outside her door. Each time it opened, Maya could see the two men sitting in chairs on either side. They held guns across their laps.

If they were there to keep her from leaving, they'd fail. As soon as she could stand, she was leaving.

Her son was alive and she had to find him.

AFTER MAKING the arrangements for Maya's protection, Shepard had waited for the guards to arrive, then he'd left the hospital. Pulling into the villa's driveway, he had little hope of finding Javier or Luisa at home, but he had to start somewhere.

He went straight to his father's bedroom and told him what had happened.

The old man stayed silent until Shepard had finished, his eyes never straying from Shepard's face. Finally he spoke. ''Which one do you think has done these evil things, Shepard? Was it Luisa or Javier?''

''I don't know, Papá.'' Shepard had been pacing

beside his father's bed but he stopped now. "What do you think?"

Eduard's hands tightened on the sheets and he pulled himself upright. His eyes flashing, he spoke with the kind of vigor he'd been missing the past few weeks. "I don't know, either. But you find out the truth, Shepard, and then you come to me! I will deal with whoever is behind this, I promise."

Shepard looked down at the man in the bed, his skepticism obvious. "Even if it's Javier?"

His father stared back with a fierce expression. "*Especially* if it's Javier. Luisa is just a woman but Javier is my son. He's a Reyes. He should know better and if he doesn't, then he will answer to me."

"And what about Mother? Her excuses for him—"

"—will cease," the old man interrupted. "If this is the truth, she will face it."

Shepard nodded at Eduard's surprising words then he left and headed for his sister's villa, his cell phone pressed against his ear as he strode through the garden. The guards reassured him that Maya was fine and his secretary repeated what she had been saying for hours: Javier was nowhere to be found. Reaching his sister's home, Shepard put away the phone then pounded on her front door. He didn't expect anyone to come to the door—each time he'd called, the housekeeper had answered him fearfully, promising Shepard Luisa had disappeared.

Rattling the doorknob, he called out, then hit the door again with a heavy fist. Someone had to be home, a maid at the very least.

When the mahogany door swung open a second later, he was shocked to see Luisa—shocked because she was there—and shocked by her appearance.

Her dark eyes were wild and haunted, her face a pasty white. She held a jacket of some sort in one hand and a bag in the other, as if she were packing. She jerked her gaze over Shepard's shoulder then brought it back. "Did you bring the police?"

His heart fell, but Shepard steeled himself. "No, I didn't bring the police. Should I go get them?"

Whirling away, she ran from him and stumbled up the stairs. Shepard closed the door behind him and followed her. He found her in her bedroom, clothes strewn from one end of the room to the other, an open suitcase on the bed.

"Are you going somewhere?"

"Leave me alone!" she screamed, throwing a sweater into the leather bag. "It was a mistake, okay! Just a mistake! All I wanted to do was scare her! I never meant to kill her!"

Shepard grabbed Luisa's arm and stopped her

frantic movements. "What did you do to Maya?" he said angrily. "What did you give her?"

She flinched and tried to pull away but he wouldn't let her. "They were herbs!" she wailed. "I put them in the tea when I knew you were coming to the mine." She continued to sob. "I made her think I was drinking the same tea but I wasn't."

"Where'd you get them?" He shook her arm. "Did Teresa give them to you? Tell me the truth!"

"Teresa?" Luisa looked at him with confusion. "*Por Dios,* no, no…why would she do something like that?"

"Did you steal them?"

"Of course not! I thought you knew already…" She shook her head, obviously more puzzled than ever. "I thought that's why you came, because you knew… Javier gave them to me."

Her words stopped him cold. "Explain."

She quickly answered him. "When Javier found out I knew about Maya, h-he said he'd h-help me. H-he gave me the h-herbs. He said to put in just a pinch and it would be enough to make her sick. I swear that's all I did." She began to cry, her makeup running down her cheeks in two dark rivers. "I never meant to kill her! I only wanted to scare her into leaving." She gripped his arms with her hands, her nails digging into his skin. "You have to believe me, Shepard. You have to—"

His sister continued to beg, but Shepard didn't

hear her. He was too busy putting the pieces of the puzzle into place. When the picture emerged, he cursed his own stupidity. He'd been right all along. Luisa had been a pawn, nothing more.

"Where is he?" He spoke so calmly, Luisa didn't hear him. Her crying went uninterrupted until he repeated his question two more times.

"Wh-where is wh-who?" she finally hiccuped.

"Where is Javier? I know he's not in Panama." Each word Shepard spoke was filled with hate. "Where is he right now?"

Luisa blinked at the harshness in Shepard's voice. "He went to Punta Perdido. He said if I handled Maya, he'd take care of her son."

MAYA WAITED until the nurse came and went, then sat up slowly, edging her legs over the side of the bed. The room spun but after a minute it came to a stop. She eased her way down until her toes hit the cold tile floor.

I can do this, she told herself, gritting her teeth. *I have to do this. I have to leave. I can't lie here. Not with my son out there somewhere...*

She made it to the foot of the bed and then her legs went out from beneath her. She broke her fall, but hit her head on the floor. She was still out when they found her.

SHEPARD DROVE straight to the airport, his cell phone pressed to his ear. The nurses told him—once more—that Maya was all right and the guards were in place. He hung up and started to make his second call but his phone rang before he could finish punching out the numbers.

The head of security's voice was regretful as it confirmed Shepard's suspicions. "I found the dozer driver," Rio said. "I don't know how to tell you this, Señor Reyes, but he was paid to start that mudslide today." He stopped, clearly reluctant to continue.

"I know the rest, Rio. Was it Luisa or Javier?"

"I'm sorry, but it was Javier. I don't understand this at all."

"You don't want to understand. And *por Dios,* I wish I didn't…"

They hung up and Shepard made his call. Teresa answered on the third ring.

He spoke without preamble. "I don't know how involved you are in what's been going on, but I have some advice for you."

"I welcome anything you have to tell me, Shepard, although I have no idea what you're talking about." Her voice was as calm as ever, her delivery slow and smooth. "I'm always open to wise counsel."

"Then find yourself a lawyer, otherwise you're going to jail."

"And why is that?"

"Because Maya's at San Joaquin. Her heart stopped. She died but the doctors brought her back."

Her sharp intake of breath sounded genuine, but he wasn't convinced. "Oh, my God. I gave her something for protection but I was afraid she wouldn't use it."

"Are you telling me you *knew* she was in danger?"

"Of course! I knew it the minute I met her at the villa."

"How did you know this, Teresa?"

"Oh, Shepard…why do you even ask that question? You have no trust of me or what I do, so whatever I say, you will not believe me."

"You're right about that," he said tightly. "So my question is, how much of a part did you play in this? Have you and Javier joined forces again? You obviously provided him the herbs. Did you give him the snake, too?"

"The snake was not the real danger." Teresa interrupted him. "You came just in time."

Shepard gripped the steering wheel. He'd told no one of Maya's encounter with Santos and his men. "There's no way you'd know that unless Javier told you."

"I have other ways of knowing things, Shepard. But I accept your distrust."

"Then accept this," he growled. "I will see you and Javier rot in hell for what you did to Maya. You will not get away with this, Teresa. None of you will. You, Javier or Luisa."

A deep silence grew at the other end of the line. "Your brother and I are not connected in any way. We share nothing. He's not a good man and I can no longer be near people like him. And as far as Luisa goes…" She stopped speaking and he heard her take a deep breath. He could almost see her white dress billowing in the wind as she stood on her patio, the bird cages falling quiet, the snakes going still. "You know as well as I that Javier merely used her."

"Are you a mind reader, too?"

"I read people's hearts, Shepard, that's all. I suggest you look deeper into your own to seek the answers you want. You're the one who's known the truth for years. You…and Renaldo. I'm going to go to the hospital now. Perhaps I can help."

She hung up the phone and Shepard did the same, an uneasy echo sounded in the back of his mind as he remembered his mother's words. Teresa had told Marisol that Renaldo had wanted to "talk" with Shepard. Was she telling Shepard she knew what he'd suspected all along?

Shepard had no idea…and in the end, it didn't matter. The outcome would be the same. Half an hour later, he arrived at the airport where the helicopter he'd ordered prepared was waiting.

Along with *his* men…and *their* guns.

MAYA COULD HEAR the nurses from her bed, the sedative they'd given her coursing through her blood. She'd tried to tell them she had to leave, but they'd ignored her pleas, trying to reassure her instead. Standing in the hallway, they were talking about her and Shepard.

"He's called three times since he's left," one said.

"*Él es tan guapo,*" another one commented. "*Y él la ama tanto…*"

Through the haze of drugs, Maya tried to correct them, at least in her mind. *He's handsome, yes, of course…but he doesn't love me. That's crazy.*

Their voices faded as they moved down the hall, the conversation continuing but without Maya's silent input.

She struggled weakly against the railings they'd raised on either side of her bed. They'd been horrified to find her on the floor and she had been, as well. She had to leave! Her son needed her.

Her eyes fluttered down, her helpless frustration giving way to confusion. And then sleep.

THEY'D NEVER FLOWN into such a tight spot. Perched on the edge of the mountains, Punta Perdido had few flat areas, much less places large enough for a helicopter landing.

Shepard's pilot wore a grimace of concentration as they circled the village and he searched for a place to touch down, dipping the aircraft repeatedly as he checked out various locations. Shepard was oblivious to the difficulty, his thoughts focused on his traitorous brother.

If Javier really had found Maya's son, the boy was already dead.

Turning to the four men sitting behind him, Shepard cautioned them once more, reiterating the most important point of the plan they'd developed as they'd flown. "There will be no gunfire until I say so," he said, his eyes meeting each man's before going to the next. "*¿Comprendes?* I want him found and detained, then you call me. I will do the rest."

"What if he shoots at us, *Jefe?*"

Shepard looked at the man sitting beside him. He was dressed in fatigues, his beard nicely trimmed, his demeanor respectful. No one would ever suspect he was a hired killer.

"Defend yourself, of course, but once you tell him I am the one who is looking for him, he will do nothing to you." Shepard felt his shoulders tighten. "My brother wants me as much as I want him."

They finally landed in what looked like the empty playground of a school. Within seconds, each man slipped silently away, their radios at their side, their weapons at the ready. Shepard headed out on his own. He'd taken the town square for himself. Javier was a lot of things, but he was no fool. He'd hear the helicopter coming in and he'd know Shepard had arrived. He'd put himself where Shepard could easily find him because that's the kind of person Javier was. He believed he was invincible and why shouldn't he? For years, he'd gotten away with everything.

Shepard's men were merely insurance.

Which immediately proved to be unnecessary.

Pausing on the edge of the square, Shepard spotted his brother at once. He was sitting at one of the cafés under a row of hanging lamps, a steaming mug in front of him, his cigar hanging from loose fingers. A pistol lay on the table before him. Shepard spoke quickly into his radio. The men would move in closer but that was all.

His own weapon cold against his back, Shepard crossed the street without hesitation and came to where his brother sat.

"What took you so long, little brother?" Javier's

dark eyes were glazed and heavy-lidded. "I've been waiting for you."

Shepard glanced at Javier then looked at the waiter who stood by the door. One glimpse of Shepard's eyes, and the man ran inside. Shepard sat down in the chair beside Javier, his gaze going to the gun then back to Javier.

"I can see that you have," he said. "I've been at the hospital. I had to take in one of *los picandoros*. There was an accident at the mine."

Javier took a sip from his coffee then drew on his cigar. "What kind of accident?"

"A mudslide. One of the dozers set it off."

"But you weren't hurt?"

"I'm here, aren't I?"

"No one else was injured, I take it?"

"Not by the mudslide."

"Oh? Did something else happen?"

"Yes," Shepard said. "Maya drank the tea spiked with the herbs you gave Luisa. What were they, Javier?"

"I have no idea." Javier shrugged as if the question barely mattered. "When I stole them from Teresa's house, I merely looked for something labeled 'poison.'"

"Well, they worked, *hermano*. Quite well."

Javier tapped the edge of his cigar on the lip of the table, the gun lying between them like a snake about to strike. "Then your lover must have died quickly. *Lo siento, mi hermano…*"

"Your apology is kind. She did die swiftly." The brothers' eyes locked at this, then Shepard spoke again. "She was at the hospital when it happened, though. And the doctors started her heart again. She's going to live." He slid his hand behind him and gripped his pistol, removing it from his waistband but keeping it out of sight. "She's going to live," he repeated. "But *you* aren't."

CHAPTER SEVENTEEN

JAVIER STARED AT HIM impassively. He'd seen Shepard's movement and understood it, but he didn't react. "You're rushing to the wrong conclusion, little brother. Luisa asked me to help her and that's all I did. She's *loco* and I had no way to stop her—"

"Luisa's role in this was meaningless. You used her, just like you used Maya's uncle. And *that's* why you are going to die."

"You don't have it in you to kill your own brother."

"You would know what it takes, wouldn't you, *hermano?*" Shepard waited for a moment, then asked the question he'd pondered for eighteen years. "What *did* it feel like to look Renaldo in the eyes and slit his throat?"

Javier stubbed out his cigar with a violent grinding motion. "Segundo Alvarez killed Renaldo."

"And you killed Segundo?"

"That's common knowledge. He was scum and he deserved to die."

"And our brother? Did he deserve to die?" Shepard's voice dropped as he continued, "Who did you murder first? Segundo or Renaldo?" He answered his own question. "Probably Segundo because he would have been on guard. Renaldo would have suspected nothing until you turned on him. He thought you were there to save him. He had no idea of your greed."

"It wasn't greed," Javier said from behind clenched teeth. "I *deserved* what they were going to give Renaldo. Me!" He hit his chest with his fist. "Me! Not him. He gave up his birthright when he chose FARC."

As his brother's anger spewed, a sad truth came to Shepard. He had never *wanted* Javier to be the man he'd suspected he was. But the truth was before him.

Shepard spoke slowly, each word painful. "With Segundo dead, no one could dispute your version of what happened. You killed our brother then told the family Maya's uncle did it." He paused. "But you didn't know Papá wouldn't change his will. And you didn't know that Renaldo had a son."

"He died," Javier insisted. "I've looked everywhere and he doesn't exist. If I can't find him, he's not alive."

"If you were sure of that, you wouldn't have tried to kill Maya."

"I wouldn't have tried to kill her if you hadn't found her first. But I knew she lived because you went to Houston. I overheard the peasant woman's story the day she came to your office so I had you watched. I tried to scare her away with the photograph but it didn't work."

A slow burn started deep inside Shepard's chest and spread outward. The mixture of guilt and regret would fuel an ache he would live with for the rest of his life. "I'm claiming the right of revenge—for Maya, for her son, and for my brother, the man she loved."

"You're out of your league, Shepard. Quit now and I'll forget we had this conversation."

"Go ahead and forget. I will remember for both of us. I will remember that you killed our brother and used our sister. I will remember that you stole from Teresa, that you put the snake in Maya's car, and that you sent Santos out to find her... I will *always* remember these things." Shepard tightened his fingers on the weapon.

In the silence that came between them, Javier stared at Shepard steadily. "You love her, don't you?" he said finally. "That's what all this is about. You love Maya Vega."

"My feelings are not the topic."

"Of course not." Javier smiled tightly. "I understand how touchy the subject could be for you. But let me give you this to think about… Have you ever asked her about her time with the rebels? Have you ever asked her about that little situation, Shepard?''

"She wasn't a *guerrillera*. Now stand up.'' Shepard jerked the barrel of the gun.

"You're right.'' Javier remained seated. "She wasn't a guerrilla. She was worse than that…'' He paused, his eyes glinting in the darkness. "She was a traitor.''

"You don't know what you're talking about.''

"I don't? Then tell me this, Shepard. How did Alvarez find Renaldo to even kidnap him in the first place? Renaldo had slipped through the Army's net for years, going in and out of the *despeje* with no one the wiser. You know that as well as I do because you met him yourself several times. At the mine, even in Bogota at the house once. Renaldo was nothing if not a ghost. How did a simple peasant like Alvarez track down Renaldo when the whole Colombian Army couldn't?''

He didn't wait for Shepard's answer.

"Our brother's lover betrayed him, that's how. She set up Renaldo because she wanted part of the money she thought her uncle would get.''

Shepard went still. From the day he'd met Maya, he'd known she had secrets. He'd seen the wall she lived behind, the mask she kept in place. Javier's words wormed their way inside Shepard's heart.

Was this what she'd been hiding? Had she played a part in Renaldo's death?

"Your precious Maya isn't the person you think she is."

Shepard refocused on his brother. "That may be true," he said softly. "But neither am I."

Raising his hand, Shepard pointed his weapon at Javier and thumbed the hammer. Javier's face blanched and in that single second, Shepard realized his brother had never expected it to go this far. He'd been so sure of himself—as always—so arrogant and self-confident, he'd assumed he could talk his way out of this as he had everything else. As the truth sank in, Javier jumped up and went for his gun.

His fingers never reached it. Shepard's men swarmed the table, the cocking of his weapon their prearranged signal. Javier's struggle was over quickly, his pistol falling uselessly from the table as he was roughly subdued and handcuffed. As the men pulled him away, his voice floated out of the darkness, his gloating attitude as defiant as ever.

"I knew you didn't have it in you, *hermano*. You could never kill me! I knew it."

Lowering his weapon, Shepard answered but only to himself. "You're right. I didn't have it in me because I am not you. *Gracias, Dio, muchas gracias*... I am *not* my brother.''

MAYA STAYED in the hospital two more days. Marisol and Eduard came the evening before she was to be released.

Marisol said little, but the old man rolled himself close to Maya's bedside and took her hand. His face was drawn yet there was a strength in his grip Maya hadn't felt before. To hasten his father's death, Javier had been adding herbs to Eduard's tea, as well. He clearly felt much better, but his eyes were full of shame as he spoke.

''I do not have the words to tell you how grieved I am for what my family has done to you. You can never forgive us, and I understand that fact.''

Maya's heart melted and she squeezed his fingers. ''You aren't responsible for what happened, Eduard. Javier was a grown man. He chose his own path.''

''But I encouraged him to take it.''

''Sometimes things like that are out of our hands.''

''Like my other son's heart? Is *it* in *your* hands?''

Maya stiffened. ''If you're speaking about Shepard, the answer is no. His heart was never there to begin with.''

''Are you sure?''

''There are very few things I'm sure of, *Señor* Reyes, but *that* is definitely one of them.''

"Then let us tell you how sorry we are about your son. If only he had lived…"

The vision she'd had of Renaldo came to her swiftly. Maya looked straight into Eduard Reyes's eyes with an unblinking stare. "Things always work out for the best."

His gaze was as sharp as hers and her heart turned over. "Do they?"

"I have no doubt about that, *señor*. None whatsoever."

The elderly couple left a little while later. The next morning as Maya dressed to leave, Shepard entered her room.

"We have doors for a reason." She coolly repeated his words to Javier. "They're there so you can knock."

In silence, he watched her button her blouse. When she finished and looked up again, he spoke. "Javier is in jail. Luisa has been released into the care of my parents. If you want to press charges—"

She waved off his suggestion. "That's not necessary."

He nodded. "They both knew who you were but Javier planned it all."

"Your mother and father told me everything."

"No, they didn't."

"What did they leave out?"

"The fact that your uncle did not kill Renaldo." Shepard took a ragged breath. "Javier killed him then blamed it on Segundo. Your uncle might not have been a good man, but he wasn't a killer, Maya. That's the whole story, I promise.''

His statement was anticlimactic. She felt nothing at the news. There was only emptiness inside her. Shepard clearly didn't share her view. Behind his expression, there was pain.

She hardened herself to his misery. All she wanted to do was get away from him and find her son. As far as she was concerned, that would be the final chapter in this sorry tale.

''None of us will ever know the *whole* story,'' she said obliquely. ''Real life doesn't work that way.'' Turning to the bed, she picked up the hairbrush one of the nurses had given her and put it on the table nearby.

''So you are leaving?''

She busied herself with her purse. ''Yes. The reservations I made last week are for Saturday. I'll keep them.''

''Let me get you a hotel room—''

She held up her hand. ''I've made my arrangements, Shepard. I don't need your help.''

''I understand, Maya. But I want to—''

''I know what you want,'' she interrupted a second time. ''It's the same thing you and your family have wanted since the beginning and that's to control everything around them.'' She shook her head.

"I may have let you get to me once, but I'm not a fool. It's not going to happen again."

He met her eyes. "So that's it? You leave, I stay, it's over? We go our separate ways and act as if what happened between us was nothing?"

"It works for me," she said.

"And if it doesn't work for me?"

"Then I'm sorry." She picked up her purse and slung it over her shoulder. "We're not going to find a compromise."

His eyes glittered with sudden anger and he began to respond. Then he tightened his mouth and kept his silence. His reaction gave her a twinge of satisfaction but it didn't feel as good as she'd expected. She started past him but all at once, his hand was on her arm, his fingers gripping her tightly.

"Don't do this to us, Maya. What we feel for each other isn't something that should be ignored. We could put the past back where it belongs and begin again."

Her traitorous heart heard his words and believed them. For a moment, she almost succumbed, then she remembered her vision. She lifted his hand from her arm and dropped it.

"You can't turn back the clock, Shepard. That's impossible...even for a Reyes."

She left the room quickly so he wouldn't see her tears. An hour later, Maya's taxi pulled into the heli-

port she and Shepard had used only three days before. A lifetime seemed to have passed since then.
She went into the office, laid down her credit card
and told them what she wanted. Within minutes, she
was in a helicopter, leaving Bogota behind.

But not her heartache. Staring out the window at
the green blur beneath, Maya could no longer contain the storm of emotions Shepard's appearance had
generated. He knew her past, knew everything about
her, had actually understood who she really was.
With him, she'd had no secrets and the relief had
been incredible. With him, she had come to understand how thick the walls she'd been hiding behind
were. She'd also come to understand why she'd
erected them in the first place. She'd wanted to protect her heart, as well as her reputation.

She'd failed.

EDUARD AND MARISOL SAT with Shepard in the living room and told their son about their visit to Maya.
They had no idea he'd seen her himself.

"She looked weak," his mother said sadly. "And
pale. Her skin is like the snow on top of the mountains. White and cold."

Shepard nodded but he wasn't really paying attention. He was thinking instead of the words he and
Maya had exchanged. They'd cut each other deeply.

"She is not happy," Eduard added. "You did her

no good by bringing her here, Shepard. You know that, don't you?''

Shepard rubbed his face with his hands then dropped them. ''*Sí*, Papá. I know that.''

''But you did the right thing.'' The old man's voice pulled Shepard's gaze up. ''And I appreciate it.''

''Do you really?'' Shepard's eyes went to his mother, who stayed silent. ''I took another son from the family. How can you thank me for that?''

''You had to do it.'' Marisol spoke for the first time and Shepard knew she meant what she said. ''I wanted Javier and Luisa to be better people so I refused to see the truth.''

''That's a mother's job,'' Shepard said.

''But the facts are the facts. You are the one who found Renaldo's real killer,'' Eduard interrupted. ''For that, we are grieved, of course, but we will always be grateful. You are a true Reyes.''

Shepard stood up from the deep leather sofa and shook his head, his gesture weary. ''A true Reyes? What is a *true* Reyes, Papá?'' He closed his eyes briefly and remembered Maya's distrust when they'd first met. He'd told her he would help her, but instead he'd turned her life upside down and had given her nothing in return. He'd never forget the way she'd looked at him in the hospital. She'd been right to distrust him and his family.

He opened his eyes. "We're killers and lunatics. Rebels and liars. I'm not sure a 'true Reyes' is what I want to be."

"It's not a choice." His father's black eyes locked on Shepard's face. "You are what you are. You can be nothing else and that will never change."

A QUIET EMPTINESS GREETED Maya in Punto Perdido when she reached the midwife's house. Undeterred, she stared through a loose shutter. There was fresh fruit on the table, she saw with relief, so they hadn't disappeared like Renita. On the flight up, Maya had been terrified that she might get here and find no one at all.

She stood on the porch of the tiny home and tried to decide what to do next. She had to find Amarilla's home in the country, but how? A thousand possibilities running through her mind, Maya didn't hear the woman behind her until she called out. Maya turned swiftly, her pulse leaping.

Holding her little boy's hand, Renita stood on the other side of the fence. She bent down to him and said something and he ran to the house next door.

Maya hurried down the sidewalk to her aunt and they came together, Renita's apology flowing between them. Maya hugged her tightly, finally soothing the other woman into a tearful silence.

"Where did you go? I came back to look for you, but you weren't here."

"I had to leave," Renita said painfully. "*Señor* Javier… he was going to hurt us, Maya. I had to go, for Juan's sake. Please forgive me…"

"I understand. It's all right… Javier's gone now. He won't be able to hurt anyone else. Not from prison."

"I know." Renita hiccuped. "Th-that's why I came back. I've been hoping you would come, too." She tilted her head toward the house. "I put the fruit on the table thinking you might see it and I asked the neighbor to look out for you. Her little boy is friends with Juan. She just sent him to me with a message that you'd come. I'm so glad, Maya."

"Are you really?"

"Oh, yes, Maya, I am. I truly am."

"Then prove it to me, *Tía*. Take me to my son because I know that he lives."

"I'll take you to Amarilla," Renita countered quietly. "She has what you want."

THE UNKEPT ROAD TWISTED and turned like a coiled snake but the man behind the wheel of the battered pickup truck didn't seem fazed by the switchbacks or the ruts. The neighbor's husband had simply nodded when Renita had knocked on their door. Leaving his wife and the two little boys standing in the doorway, they'd been off five minutes after that, heading out of town.

Amarilla lived ten miles away, her farm well hidden in the mountains, Renita had explained cryptically. As they rose higher and higher, the forest growing dense, Maya decided the midwife's crop was probably illegal.

No matter how strongly the government denied it, Colombia's economy depended on the coca trade as much as the rebels depended on their guns. And the two were as inextricably linked now as they had been when Renaldo had been alive. They were driving straight into rebel country. If Amarilla farmed here, she raised coca and sold it to FARC. They, in turn, traded it for guns.

Maya's thoughts flew out the window as the driver slammed on the brakes. She gasped and beside her, Renita put out a hand, saving herself from hitting the dashboard at the very last minute. A man stood before them in the center of the road, their bumper inches from his knees. He held an automatic weapon.

Stepping slowly to the driver's side of the car, he stared at them with a menacing look, then his eyes went to Renita's. Clearly recognizing her, he nodded once and stepped aside.

"Wh-what did he want?" Maya stuttered as they started up again.

"He checks everyone," Maya's aunt said. "It's for the best." Looking out the rear window of the truck, she returned to the silence she'd maintained the whole trip.

A few miles down the road, a clearing opened up before them, a small farmhouse situated in the center, various outbuildings spread out behind it.

The midwife's daughter opened the door before they even knocked, obviously alerted by the guard at the checkpoint.

"It's all right, Maria," Renita said firmly. "Your mother's expecting us."

The girl looked uncertain until someone came up behind her and spoke softly. Immediately, she bowed her head and stepped to one side.

Maya caught her breath. The woman who'd held her hand all those years ago had aged badly, time weighing on her like a heavy load. Standing with a bent back, her hair completely white, Amarilla seemed ancient. Only her eyes had any substance, their depths deep and sad.

The woman held the door open for Maya and Renita to enter. Maya wasted no time. "I've come for the truth, Amarilla. I know my son lived. Where is he?"

Instead of answering, the midwife turned and began to hobble down the hallway, leaving Maya no choice except to follow. Renita trailed behind. They entered a wide corridor and walked to the end of the hall. Amarilla stopped beside a door, her hand on the knob, and looked at Renita, speaking for the first time. "Did you tell her?"

Renita shook her head and Amarilla's eyes went to Maya. "How did you figure it out?"

Maya explained part of what she'd realized at the hospital. The midwife had just one daughter. She'd been born late, Amarilla giving birth to her two weeks before Maya had gone into labor herself. "I remembered you had your daughter just before I had my own child..." Maya licked her lips nervously. "She has no twin brother."

Without saying a word, the old woman opened the door beside them. Maya sent a puzzled look toward Renita but her aunt's face was a mask. A catch formed in Maya's chest. She couldn't be wrong, could she?

The small sitting room was decorated simply and Maya immediately knew this was the heart of the home, Amarilla's private domain. She waved them toward a sofa then sat down herself, in a padded armchair, her movements slow and painful. When she was settled, she looked up. "I delivered hundreds of babies but I couldn't conceive myself. I'd given up hope, then she came."

"But she came alone."

"You're right," Amarilla confirmed. "She had

no twin. The boy she thinks is her brother was *your* child.''

Maya's heart felt as if it were going to explode and she suddenly feared it might stop again. She forged ahead as if she didn't care. ''You told me he died, but you took him.''

''Yes, I did,'' Amarilla said. ''I drugged your son to make him look dead then I took him and I raised him.''

Maya didn't know if she should laugh or cry. ''Where is he? Is he here? I want to see him—''

''Later.'' The old woman's command was stern.

Maya started to argue then realized she wouldn't win. She gave an order of her own. ''Then tell me why,'' she said. ''Why did you do this to me?''

Renita answered instead of Amarilla. ''I feared for the baby's safety.''

''Why?''

''Segundo was an evil man,'' Renita said. ''Evil and stupid. He told me he didn't want to care for another child who wasn't his own, but there was more to it than that. I'd overheard him bragging about his plans. He was going to collect a ransom for Renaldo, then get even more for the baby.'' She made a sound Maya couldn't decipher. ''If I'd known he was never coming back, how different this would have turned out…''

Maya grew still, Luisa's words echoing in her mind. "He didn't return because he was killed."

"Yes. Thank God, he was killed." Renita's voice was nothing but factual. "I guess his plans went wrong. I never knew what happened, except that both of them died."

"I don't understand... Renaldo was smart and fast. How could Segundo have ever grabbed him?"

"Renaldo didn't know he was meeting Segundo." Renita dropped her gaze. "He thought he was meeting you...because that's what Segundo told him."

The words pierced Maya with disbelief then guilt.

Reading her mind, the old woman put her hand on Maya's arm. "Don't hold yourself responsible, Maya. Renaldo knew what kind of man Segundo was. He had warned me before the birth that if anything happened, I was to protect the child. And that's what I did."

"*I* could have protected him!" Maya said thickly. "*I* could have raised him."

"No, you couldn't have," Amarilla said bluntly. "With me, the boy's identity was safe. With you, who knows what would have happened?"

Maya turned to her aunt. "If that's the case, then why did you go to Shepard? You knew he'd find me. Was the story about thanking him for helping your son just that? A story?"

The two older women exchanged a look at Maya's question and the fist around her heart tightened.

"I did want to thank Sr. Shepard but I went to him for a different reason," Renita confirmed slowly. "It wasn't about your son, though…"

Maya looked from her aunt to the midwife, her confusion mixing with an unexplainable fear.

"Your son, Emilio, grew up to be a rebel, just like the girl he loved. Just like his father." Amarilla's voice quivered. "And he was killed two months ago in a raid."

Maya stared at the woman without comprehension, the words she'd just uttered too much to take in. Her son had been named Emilio and now he was dead? Maya shook her head back and forth, her voice cracking. "No," she said slowly. "No, no, no. I don't believe you… Renaldo told me he needed me. I—I saw Renaldo when I died and he said—" She turned to Renita. "Tell me she's lying," she demanded. "Tell me!"

Renita dabbed her own eyes. "It's true, *pobrecita.* I'm sorry, but it's true. Emilio and his girlfriend are both gone. She fought beside him and she died there, as well."

Maya half stood, then sat back down. Her pulse throbbed then seemed to stop. She shook her head. "I can't believe this. Not after everything that's happened... How can you lose a child twice in one lifetime?''

A wave of grief and anger swamped her, taking away the little control she had left. She began to cry. All she had wanted was to hold her son. Just once. He would have been eighteen, but surely he would have allowed her this one thing. A simple hug. She dropped her head, her sobs tugging at her body. Renita patted her back and cried beside her.

Amarilla spoke softly. ''I can't replace him,'' she said sadly, ''but I can help heal your pain.''

Maya answered, her voice broken with sorrow. ''No one can do that.''

Without a word, the midwife turned and called to her daughter. The young girl came so quickly Maya knew she had to have been waiting just outside the door.

In her arms, she held a baby.

''Someone has to stop this madness.'' Standing painfully, Amarilla took the child from her daughter then held him out to Maya. ''This is Emilio's son— your grandchild, Maya Vega. Take him and raise him right. Let him know a world better than this one.''

MAYA LEFT COLOMBIA on Saturday. Exactly one week before, Shepard had held her in his arms and made love to her all night long. Now she was leaving and he'd never see her again.

Standing by one of the windows in the airport, Shepard watched her get on the plane. She chatted with the man in front of her, then turned and spoke to a woman behind her who held a child, shooting a quick glance back to the waiting area as she did so. Shepard's pulse jumped. For a second, he thought she might have seen him. But she continued inside the plane.

Thank God.

He'd done nothing but hurt Maya, and she didn't deserve that. She was an extraordinary woman, a loving woman, who had cared more about doing the right thing than she had ever cared about herself.

He watched until the aircraft was nothing but a dot in the bright Colombian sky.

CHAPTER EIGHTEEN

PATRICIA LEANED BACK against Maya's sofa and shook her head. "My God, Maya. I don't know what to say. I'm in shock. When you called from Bogota and asked me to help you with the Immigration people, I was curious, but I had no idea…"

Maya gave the cradle beside her another push and sent it gently rocking. Without the law firm pulling some important strings, both in Houston and in Bogota, she doubted she would have been able to bring her precious gift back with her.

"How could I have explained all this over the phone, Patricia? You would have thought I'd lost my mind. You wouldn't have believed me." Maya glanced down at the sleeping baby and thought of the dream she'd had in the hospital. The man she'd seen had not been Renaldo, but her *son.*

"I can hardly believe it myself," she added softly.

"Well, I'm astonished," Patricia reiterated. "Simply astonished. But I'm proud of you, too. Very, very proud."

"Even though I'm giving up the race for the judgeship?"

"Your search turned up more than just a child, Maya. It uncovered your true priorities. The judgeship is nothing in comparison."

"I was afraid I'd disappointed you."

"Maya, darling, you could never disappoint me. That would be impossible." Patricia's gray eyes darkened with a pain that was usually well-hidden. "You made the right decision. Nothing is more important than family and don't you ever forget that. If I'd had children, I would have left the firm in a heartbeat and never looked back. You're doing the right thing, believe me."

Maya crossed the room and sat down next to her friend. "I appreciate the vote of confidence, Patricia, but after I saw him, I didn't have a choice. I would have died before I'd left Colombia without Luis."

"And what about the Reyeses? Have you made up your mind for certain?"

"Yes, I have." Maya's mouth went tight with determination. "They know nothing about him and it's staying that way."

"Is that fair?"

"Not at all." Maya thought of Eduard and Marisol, then closed her mind. "But that's how it's going to be."

"And what about Shepard? It's going to get tough, you know."

"What do mean?"

"Pretending you don't love someone is a hard act to maintain, Maya. You'll grow tired of it."

"I *don't* love him. He used me, just like his brother used his sister. He should have told me the truth about everything from the very beginning, whether he was absolutely sure or not. I should have known."

"You're absolutely right." Patricia sighed and rose from the couch, smoothing her skirt as she stood. "As always. But really, the whole situation boils down to a question that no one can answer...except you."

Maya lifted her eyes. "And what is that?"

"Do you want to be right or do you want to be loved?"

Patricia's point stayed with Maya long after the other woman left, and the following morning she was still thinking about it. When Maya saw how gorgeous the weather was she dressed the baby and got the stroller out, hoping a walk would clear her head.

At the park a block away from her house, Maya pushed the stroller to a bench and sat down. The last time she'd been in this kind of setting she'd been with Shepard, denying the possibility that her son had ever lived past his dangerous birth. Words couldn't describe how happy she was that she'd been wrong yet grief still stayed near. She glanced at her grandchild. The midwife had told her Luis looked exactly like Maya's son had at that age.

To Maya, Luis looked exactly like Shepard.

She closed her eyes and let a tiny groan escape. When Patricia had questioned her about Shepard, it'd taken more strength than Maya had to deny her love for him. She'd had to, though, because if she admitted to the truth, she'd be lost.

She *couldn't* love him and raise her grandchild, too.

Shepard had proven to her more than once that he truly was a Reyes. If he ever found out about Luis, Shepard would want to take the baby away even though he wasn't the child they'd sought. He'd want him brought up in Colombia. And that was something Maya could never, ever let happen. She hadn't saved this child from a life with the rebels to be brought up in the Reyes tradition. To her way of thinking, one was as bad as the other.

Leaning over, she picked up Luis, her hand smoothing his hair before she dropped a kiss on his forehead, the sweet smell of baby powder filling her senses as she cradled him in her arms. The possibility that Shepard would ever find out about the baby was remote at best. He had no clue Luis even existed and he would probably never seek out Maya again.

What they'd had was over.

SHEPARD WAITED for his pulse to slow and his breathing to return to normal. By the time that happened, he thought he'd be able to understand the sight before him. Until then, he wasn't sure he could make any sense of it at all.

What was Maya doing with a baby?

Too little time had passed for the child to be his and too much time had passed for the child to be hers.

From his car, he watched her and the baby for almost ten minutes, her every moment making it more and more clear that she wasn't simply babysitting for someone. The child in her arms was one she loved.

He gripped the steering wheel and tried to decide what to do. He hadn't planned on this.

Then again, he hadn't planned on anything that had happened in the past few weeks. When his father's words had finally sunk in, Shepard had known he had to take action. *You are what you are. You can be nothing else and that will never change.*

His last name might be Reyes, but his path was not preordained.

He'd promptly given control of the mine back to

his now healthy father and left. He wanted his own life and leaving Colombia was one way he could get it.

But that life wouldn't be worth having if Maya was not by his side. He'd acknowledged that fact shortly after she'd left. Going over everything that had happened, he'd remembered Javier's words about her betraying Renaldo, words he'd forgotten until that moment. With sudden surety, Shepard had known—*known in his heart*—that Javier had been lying. He didn't know how Segundo had captured Renaldo, but Maya hadn't been a part of it. She wasn't that kind of woman and never had been.

He reached into the pocket of his jacket and touched the emerald necklace he'd had made for her. The stone had been the one the old miner had found right before the mudslide. The treasure hunter had asked Shepard about it while he was still recovering. In the confusion that had followed the accident, Shepard had forgotten about the stone. The piece had turned out as perfect as he'd expected. His eyes went back to the woman on the bench.

The woman and the baby.

Without further thought, he pushed open the car door and made his way across the park. Occupied with the infant, Maya didn't look up until his shadow fell across her.

Shock rolled over her face, then fear replaced it.

Her reaction was so stark and raw, it made Shepard
hurt for her. And then for himself. How had he
turned into a man who could instill such emotion in
a woman? She hugged the child to her chest and
stared up at him, her dark eyes as compelling as the
first time he'd seen her and just as distrustful as the
last time they'd talked.

"What are you doing here?"

"I came to see you. We have a conversation to
finish." He dropped his eyes to the now sleeping
baby. "Who is this?"

She usually had the ability to hide her reactions
but not this time.

His voice went soft. "Please tell me the truth,
Maya. Whatever it is, we'll deal with it. I promise."

"Your promises are worthless."

"You're right," he conceded. "They have been.
But not anymore. Please...tell me about the child."

Her grip tightened on the baby. "Why do you
want to know?"

He dropped to the bench at her side and took her
hand in his. "Do you really have to ask that question?"

"Of course I do. And you have to answer it, too."

"I love you, Maya. That's why I'm here and
that's why I want to know. Nothing you can say or
do will make that fact change so you might as well
tell me."

"You love me?" Skepticism deepened her voice. "Do you even know what love is?"

"Probably not." He sighed and caught the surprise in her eyes. "I do know what it isn't, though."

She waited.

He twined their fingers together. "It isn't something you give to someone simply because you're related. Or because you think you should. Or even because you *want* to give it away. Love is none of those things. It comes on its own and leaves the same way."

"Has it come to you or left?"

"Both." He reached over and drew his finger down the baby's face, then he looked up at Maya. "When I located you and we searched for your son, I found your love. But when you left, I lost it, as well. I'm here because I love you, and I'll do anything I can in order to prove that fact to you."

"Anything?" Her voice trembled.

"Absolutely anything. No reserves."

She glanced down at the baby then brought her gaze back to Shepard. "Would you walk away from me," she whispered, "and never look back?"

"Is that what you want?"

"Would you do it?" she insisted.

"If that is what you truly desire, then I will." He leaned closer. "But I'd rather cut out my heart. It'd be easier and less painful but still give you the same results.''

Her eyes filled with tears. Two slid down her cheeks unimpeded, finally landing on the baby's blanket. Shepard brushed them away with his thumb, then he lifted her chin to stare into her eyes.

''I've given up everything to come here and be with you. The mine, my home, my family…I've left it all. I walked away to start a new life with you.'' He took his fingers away and looked at her. ''If you want me to give you up, as well, I will,'' he continued softly. ''But nothing will be left after that.''

She struggled to get her emotions under control. When she'd accomplished that task, she leaned over and put the sleeping baby back into the stroller. Her movements were so gentle, he never even stirred. Sitting back, she looked over Shepard's shoulder and into the distance, a series of expressions crossing her face. Finally her eyes returned to his.

''There's something you have to know about this child but before I tell you what it is, I'm going to make you promise me one thing.'' Her voice was fierce. ''If you can't do it, then you have to walk away.''

''Whatever it is, I promise.''

''Don't say that,'' she warned. ''The price might be too high.''

''Then ask it.''

"You have to promise you'll never take this child from me." Her eyes hardened. "No matter what."

Shepard frowned, his puzzlement clear. "Why would I want to do that?"

"Will you give me your word or not?"

"I love you, Maya, more than life itself." He took both her hands in his and held them tight. "And I swear—on *that* love—that I will never take this child from you."

She hesitated another heartbeat, then she started to speak, her words coming out with painful slowness. "This is going to sound strange, but when I was in the hospital—I had a dream. I saw a man I thought was Renaldo."

Shepard's expression registered his shock, but Maya continued. "It wasn't him, though. I went back to Punto Perdido and found out the truth."

She took a deep breath. "The man I saw was my son, Emilio. He and his girlfriend were *los rebeldes,* just like Renaldo. But they were killed two months ago. That's why Renita came to you in the first place. She wanted you to find me so I could raise *his* son."

A thousand questions flooded Shepard's mind. Maya saw them in his eyes because she held up her hand. "The details can come later. What's important right now is this child." She looked over at the sleeping baby. "He's a Reyes, Shepard. But he's my grandson. And I'm going to raise him myself."

All at once, Shepard understood. No other explanation was necessary.

"You aren't going to raise him yourself," he said quietly. "*We're* going to raise him…*together.* You and I. We can explain the circumstances to him when he's old enough to understand. He can make his own decisions after that."

Reaching out, Shepard pulled Maya into his arms and kissed her deeply. She filled more than his embrace, she filled his entire world and he tried to tell her that with his lips. When he lifted his head, her eyes were dazed but she still managed to question him.

"Are you sure you want to do that, Shepard? A child is a huge commitment—"

"I wouldn't have made the offer unless I meant it, Maya." He tightened his arms around her. "The only question that remains is whether or not you'll let me stay in your life. I love you beyond belief, but it's your choice now. One way or the other, I want you to have this."

He pulled the necklace from his jacket and held it out to her. A ray of sunlight came over his shoulder and hit the emerald, turning it into green fire. She blinked at its brilliance, then she took the piece from his fingers and placed it around her neck. A moment later she kissed him in a way Shepard knew he'd never forget. When it finished, she kept her hands on either side of his face and looked deep into his eyes. "It's beautiful and I love it. But I love you even more."

He smiled and brought her to him, kissing her one more time. "Does this mean the search is over?"

She glanced toward the sleeping baby then brought her eyes back to his. "My search *is* over. I found everything I'll ever need…and much, much more."

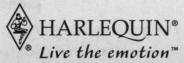

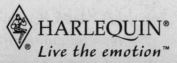

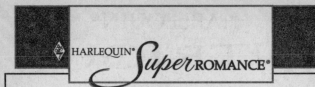

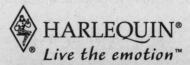

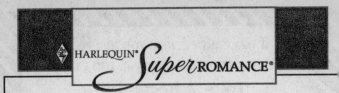

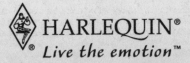